Once a Prompt a Time

Stories Sparked by Quirky Contest Prompts

Laurie O'Connor Stephans

This is a work of fiction. All incidents and dialogue, and all characters (except for any well-known historical figures) are products of the author's imagination and are not to be construed as real. Where real-life historical figures appear, the situations, incidents, and dialogues concerning those persons are entirely fictional and are not intended to depict actual events or to change the entirely fictional nature of the work. In all other respects, any resemblance to actual persons, living or dead, events, or locales is entirely coincidental.

Peggy's Library Card Publishing

First paperback printing: March 2026

First hardcover printing: July 2026

ISBN: 979-8-9950576-0-4

~ Dedication ~

For my parents,
Peggy and Vince O'Connor.

They never stopped
encouraging me in life,
and continue to be an inspiration
from the great beyond.

~ Introduction ~

Once upon a time there was a writer who had trouble writing anything without a deadline. [Spoiler alert: that hasn't changed much.] That's fine when you're a journalist but it's a big stumbling block when you want to expand into the world of creative writing.

That writer, of course, is me. And yet here you are, holding a collection of forty-four short stories written by yours truly. Not ideas. Not notes. Not half-done and abandoned. Forty-four complete short stories. How in the world did that happen?

Simple. I discovered writing contests. A little more than ten years ago I entered my first contest and was instantly hooked. Most contests have entry fees, and all have very strict deadlines. That was the perfect formula for someone who works best at the last minute under pressure and who is too cheap to give up when she has forked over money.

Besides a portfolio, writing for contests has given me something even more important—an exposure to genres I rarely read and would never have considered writing. That's why these stories, which range from one hundred to three thousand words, run the gamut from comedy to horror and most everything in between. Being forced out of my literary comfort zone has made me a better reader *and* writer.

Each story includes the specific prompt I had to follow, but I've put it at the end of the story to avoid spoilers as well as to explain some of the ridiculous things you may come across as you are reading. Eccentric vampire? A body bag? Five words that end in "ice"? Culinary catastrophe? You find all of them here… and more!

I will caution here that some of the subject matter and writing is intense and graphic. Once again to avoid spoilers, I have not included trigger warnings on specific stories. As with all adult fiction, should you find certain topics or language to be offensive or triggering, I invite you to simply move on the next story.

If you are a lover of fiction or short stories, I thank you for choosing this book from among the infinite possibilities at your disposal and hope it lives up to—or exceeds—your expectations.

And if you've found this book as a writer, I offer the added hope that my examples and experience prove inspirational in your own writing journey, and I look forward to reading your own work someday.

Thank you for joining me on this journey. I hope it takes you to new and wonderful places along the way.

All the best,

Laurie

~ Table of Contents ~

Family Dynamics and Homemade Banana Bread

Janet stretched on her tiptoes to reach the last ornament on the tree. Tiny hands had done their best to follow the still-visible-in-places lines to cut a bright yellow star from construction paper, with "2014" scrawled in green crayon in the middle. It was glued to a paper doily, laminated, and hole-punched for its festive red yarn for hanging.

She turned it over, but the doily obscured the artist's signature on the back of the star. Based on the year and ability level, Janet figured it was the work of then seven-year-old Nathan, the fourth of her six children.

Taking down the Christmas decorations was an all-day affair for Janet. While some people—including her sisters—tried to replicate magazine layouts with their precisely color-coordinated displays of store-bought finery, Janet preferred the nostalgia of homemade ornaments accumulated over the more than twenty-five years she and Ted had been married.

So, as each glitter-shedding ball and aluminum foil candy cane was placed carefully in the storage box, Janet took a moment to revel in the memories each one stirred. Every year the tradition became a bit more melancholy as her children aged along with the mementos.

Her oldest two were grown and flown, and Caroline would do the same when she finished college this year. The other three were in high school, which meant it would be just a blink of the eye before they had an empty nest.

Janet placed the lid on the last box and looked around the room. All that was left was the pile of Christmas cards, photos, and letters in the box on the mantel. She refilled her coffee cup, grabbed the box, and sat down on the sofa for the final ritual.

She'd heard electronic greetings had replaced traditional Christmas cards, but not so among their friends and *most* of their family. There were dozens of the kinds of cards she'd seen her whole life—nothing fancy, and roughly a fifty-fifty mix of Santa and baby Jesus. Envelopes were hand-written, along with personalized messages inside. Some senders—mostly family—also included the traditional year-in-review Christmas letter, in which children's accomplishments were lauded and medical procedures described in much-too-graphic detail.

Janet re-read everything before putting the cards and letters in the "toss" pile, occasionally keeping an enclosed photo to put on the fridge. Her sisters had opted to go with one of those services that prints and mails your family picture and generic greeting.

Linda, the oldest of the three and a successful attorney in Georgia, posed with her husband, Roger, and their son on a bright fall day in front of Georgetown Law School. Roger Parkland III, was in his second year, following in the footsteps of both his parents.

Middle sister Susan, a high-level vice president at a worldwide financial firm based in Manhattan, chose a seasonal photo for her automated card. She, architect husband James, and medical resident daughter Joanna, were in full ski gear from last winter's vacation in the Italian Alps.

No need to brag, girls. Mom takes care of that for you every year.

Janet set the photo cards on the fridge pile, picked up her mother's Christmas letter, and began reading. She skipped over the bursitis and Garden Club updates and went straight to the breaking news about the family.

But enough about me and my silly aches and pains. So much has happened with the girls and their children, I could just burst with pride!

Linda and Roger are still in Atlanta. Roger is running for a local judge spot, and Linda was just made partner at her firm. Little Roger is going to have big shoes to fill when he gets out of law school!

Susan, once again, was named in the Top 100 Women in Finance in the whole country! James was just named lead architect on a new skyscraper in New York, and Joanna is halfway through her third year of residency in a big hospital in Connecticut. She has delivered six babies already, and that's not even going to be her specialty!

Which brings me to my baby, Janet, and her babies. Both Teddy Jr. and Jenna work and live in Chicago. She is doing something with computers, and he is a salesman for an insurance company. Caroline is in her senior year at Northern and is going to do something in Marketing. Nathan, Olivia, and David are all in high school! It's so great they are here in town so I can watch their sports games and plays and so on. And Ted still tells people he's the best auto mechanic in Somonauk. Of course, he's the only one in our village of 1,800 people, so he's right! And Janet keeps busy with volunteering at church and keeping the house in order with all the activity there. She still makes the best banana bread of anyone I've ever known!

Linda's a partner in a law firm, Susan's managing the world's money, and Mom can only brag about my banana bread and housekeeping. And she's practically in the delivery room with Joanna, but Jenna does "something with computers." She's an IT manager at a loop firm! I guess her disappointment in me can't help but carry over to the kids.

Janet gathered everything and started for the kitchen when her cell rang. It was Ted.

"How's the best mechanic in Somonauk?" she quipped. "You know that's pretty high praise coming from—" Ted interrupted her.

"Erwin just called me. It's your mom."

Erwin was the Village Police Chief. Janet dropped the cards and photos and grabbed the back of a chair.

"I'm sorry, honey," Ted continued. "She was at Garden Club and collapsed. They called the squad, and they tried to revive her, but, well, she's gone. I'm so sorry."

Janet heard the words, but it took a few seconds for them to unscramble in her brain.

"Honey?" Ted asked.

"Where is she now?"

"They took her to Sandwich Hospital. I guess that's protocol. The coroner will meet us there. I'll close the shop and be home in ten minutes to pick you up." He paused. "I'm sorry to tell you on the phone, but word gets around so fast, I didn't want you to hear it from anyone else."

"No, that was the right thing to do," Janet said. "I'll call Linda and Susan while I'm waiting for you. Thanks, Ted. I love you."

"Love you too."

***

It was the first time since her father's funeral twelve years earlier that all of them were together at the farm. Just as the committal ended at the cemetery, a heavy, wet snow began to fall, and they had been lucky to navigate back to the homestead to settle in for the night.

The octet of cousins—after a lengthy debate at Grandma's game cupboard—had settled around the giant country kitchen table after finally agreeing on Monopoly. It was far enough away from the front room that shouts of "you were the top hat the last time" could be heard but didn't interfere with the adult conversation.

As in most homes, the fireplace was the focal point of the room, and the translucent rainbow of roaring flames was a living masterpiece to behold. Janet looked at her sisters and brothers-in-law, all of them transfixed by the fire.

"Don't they have fire in the big city?" she asked, breaking their spell.

"We have three fireplaces in our condo," James said, "but they are all gas. Honestly, I've never seen anything like this."

"It's the memories it brings back for me," Linda said. "Remember that big blizzard and cold spell when we were in grade school? I bet we had three feet of snow. The roads were impassable and school was closed for a whole week. We ran out of propane, and the trucks couldn't get through, so we all slept in sleeping bags on the floor right here in front of the fire."

"I don't know how she did it, but Mom had to cook in the fireplace too," Janet said. "It was like something from *Little House on the Prairie*, except I don't think they had s'mores."

"Then the well froze, so we had to bring in snow to melt to flush the toilet," Susan said, as animated as if she were still nine years old.

"It wasn't just for the toilets," Janet reminded them. "Mom needed it to cook and for everyone to drink. Remember the chant?"

"Oh my God, yes," Linda said. "All together now:"

"Watch out where the huskies go, and don't you eat that yellow snow!"

This started a fifteen-minute bout of contagious laughter; just when it seemed the women had regained their composure, one of them would start again and set off the others.

Once it had well and truly passed, Janet offered to refill drinks as Susan's phone chimed.

"Looks like our snow days are going to be more than a trip down memory lane," Susan said. "O'Hare and Midway just announced a ground stop through at least tomorrow, and since there's no sign of the snow letting up, it might last a couple days."

"I don't know how Wall Street and the judicial system will manage without the two of you, but I'm glad we're getting extra time together," Janet said. "And at least its not too cold out, so we don't have to worry about the well."

"Not too cold?" Linda said. "I'm sitting the closest to the fire and I still can't get warm."

"Why I declare you have turned into just a delicate magnolia blossom, bless your heart," Susan teased, affecting a perfect southern drawl.

"If I recall," Janet added, "weren't you the one who dared everybody—and led the way—to go streaking at Julie MacDonald's 12th birthday party in January?"

"Who went streaking?" a voice yelled from the kitchen.

"You just play Monopoly and mind your own business," Linda yelled back. "Holy shit, they must have gotten their hearing from Mom."

"Don't worry, Linda," Janet said. "Mom has plenty of blankets here and the propane truck just came last week. I bet I can even find some of her long underwear if you are desperate."

"It may come to that," Linda said. "But I'll start with the antifreeze that I know works best. Fill 'er up!"

Linda held out her glass and Roger filled it with brandy. Everyone seemed to sigh in unison as they settled deeper into their respective overstuffed sofa or chair, as if a pack of dogs who had each expertly circled before settling into the perfect spot and position.

***

Two days later, the storm had ended, roads were clear and the airports reopened. Although everyone was anxious to get back to their real lives, there was a genuine sadness when the time came to say goodbye.

"Let's not wait until someone is dead before we get together again," Susan said. "We'd love to have YOU visit us in New York. We could do the whole touristy thing and see a Broadway play or a Rangers game at Madison Square Garden."

"Well, we'd love *y'all* to come to Atlanta too," Linda said. "No long underwear needed, and Roger makes a killer mint julep!"

Everyone promised to make it happen one place or the other, and Janet, who was the executor of the estate, promised to be in touch once she spoke to their mother's lawyer. Before she knew it, her sisters and their families had driven off in their rental cars and, even with eight people still in the house, it somehow felt kind of empty.

Everyone pitched in to clean up after the extended sleepover, and they made the short trip back to their house. Jenna and Teddy still had one more day of bereavement leave, so they agreed on a big family dinner and their own game night before they went home and Caroline went back to school.

After a scrumptious fried chicken dinner, they cleared the table and began the debate about what to play. Janet and Ted vetoed Monopoly, and after much discussion they landed on Uno.

"It's been a long time since you've seen your cousins," Janet said as Ted dealt the first hand. "They've sure lived a different life from you guys." She hesitated, then added, "Does that ever bother you?"

"Why would it bother us?" Jenna said. "I mean, yeah, they've had a lot of luxuries and traveled and stuff, but it kind of came at a price."

Caroline and Teddy nodded; Janet didn't understand.

"What price?"

"They both were sent to boarding school before they were even teenagers," Caroline said. "Don't you remember that?"

"Yes, but that seemed like a great educational opportunity."

"Mom, they were miserable," Jenna said. "Don't you remember that Joanna and I were pen pals when we were like twelve or thirteen?"

"I do kind of remember that."

"She did nothing but complain in her letters. She was away from home, and lonely. The teachers and room mothers or whatever were ridiculously strict. She got her first period the first month she was there—"

"Ew," David said.

"Grow up; you're in high school," Jenna said, "and draw four, yellow."

She turned back to her mom. "Anyway, when Jenna told the room mother what happened she just told her, 'Supplies are in the bathroom closet' and left it at that. Jenna didn't need a room mother; she needed a real one.

"Every letter she told me how she couldn't wait to grow up and move away because Aunt Susan and Uncle James had made it clear their careers were more important to them than she was. And that she was so jealous of our normal family and how great you and Dad were."

"You know Roger doesn't want to be a lawyer," Teddy said, putting down a Reverse card. "He's just doing it because it's been expected of him since he was a little kid. He hated the boarding schools, too.

"He said the best times of his childhood were when theY visited in the summer and dad showed him how to work on the car. I wouldn't be a bit surprised if he gets through law school and then decides to be a mechanic. He just needs to get the nerve to tell Aunt Linda and Uncle Roger."

Janet was dumbstruck.

All this time I thought my kids were missing out on the good life. I had no idea.

"Uno!" Olivia screamed, bringing Janet back to the game. Once more around the table and Olivia was out. Janet stood up.

"Deal me out this hand; I'm going to get dessert."

***

The following week, after normal life had resumed, Janet saw her mother's lawyer. He provided copies of the death certificate as well as a filed copy of the will and went over the process to manage the estate. Because the farm was in a trust, there Was be no need for probate, and his office would be able to assist in the administration of the trust estate.

"You should be very grateful to your mother," he said. "She made sure her estate documents were in order to make things as easy as possible for you and the other heirs when the time came. Not all parents do that."

"I certainly am grateful and thank you for your time and assistance as well," Janet said. She stood to go.

"There's one more thing," the lawyer said. He reached into the folder and pulled out an envelope. "This is a letter your mother wrote to you. I was asked to deliver it directly."

"She wrote each of us a letter?"

"No," he said. "Only you."

***

Janet sat in the same chair where she had re-read her mother's Christmas letter just weeks earlier. Her hands trembled a bit as she opened the envelope and read the final message from her mom.

My darling Janet,

I have always tried to treat you and your sisters equally, and to never treat any of you differently or as my favorite. Officially, I maintain that position, and if you ever tell anyone (even Ted) otherwise I promise to come back and haunt you! Because, my darling, I now confess that you are and always have been my favorite.

Why tell you now? Well, as you know, I also had two sisters. They both moved away as soon as they could to make their fortunes, and I stayed on the farm in sleepy little Somonauk to marry a good local man and have a family. I always felt that my sisters, and even my parents, looked down on me as less than. I felt for a long time that I'd disappointed everyone. It wasn't until I was much older that I realized I had made the best choice of all.

Now, I don't say that your sisters think that of you, and to be sure, your father and I never, ever did either. But I have sometimes seen in your eyes that you might feel as I did. So, I want you to learn—much earlier than I did—that YOU are the most successful of your sisters. I made a fuss about them, because their egos needed it. Everyone who knows you already knows how great you are.

You are a caring and decent person. Like me, you married a great man who loves and cares for you and his children and doesn't put on airs. Your children are respectful and know what the truly important things in life are. You have done a wonderful job, and before it was too late, I wanted you to know it.

So, my darling. Keep up the good work. Your father and I will be looking down on you with pride until we see you again.

Love,
Mom

P.S. I'm not kidding about the haunting! XOXOXO

Janet put the letter back in its envelope and tucked it into her apron pocket. She wiped tears from her eyes, went into the kitchen, and pulled out her mixing bowl.

This was going to be the best banana bread she had ever made.

~ The Prompt ~

Category: Short Story

Character:
Someone who feels like
the black sheep of the family

Setting: A snow day

Must include: A well

Someone Old, Someone New

Nobody wants surprises on their wedding day.
But sometimes the worst surprise can lead to a bigger, and even better one.

Like-minded single people fill the steps of City Hall.
For somehow, they had mustered the required wherewithal
to tie the knot, to take the plunge, to say the big "I do."
And get their mothers off their backs…
          alone, that's worth the queue.

The doors at last are opened, making nervous couples smile.
So, two by two they enter forming one long wedding aisle.

An Uber stops just down the street, a frantic groom inside.
A block away a taxi brings an agitated bride.
Their other halves will give them hell because
          they're running late,
so both take off at breakneck speed, as from a starting gate.

They scale the steps in unison, and both take in the view.
"My fiancé must be inside," she says; he nods, "Mine, too."
He holds the door, she steps inside, and both survey the room.
Despite its overwhelming cheer, each feels a sense of gloom.

There are no other single folks; each person has a mate.
They fear they've been forgotten like that sock the dryer ate.
Their circumstance creates a bond, a feeling they can't hide,
so rather than sit separately they plop down side-by-side.

At first, they're duty-bound to think that something isn't right.
They text and call and watch the door, but soon
they see the light.

Concern gives way to anger. "Oh, I want to make him pay!"
"Agreed," he says, "let's brainstorm. The games are underway!"
They verbalize their fantasies to torture and impale,
but change the subject when they fear they might end up in jail.

They people watch the couples—each unique and yet the same.
To keep their mind off other things they play a little game.
Who's older? Who is younger? Is she pregnant or just fat?
Will those two last the winter? Will she let him keep his cat?

"I can't stay mad," she tells him, "or I'll surely go insane.
"I still would like to kill him, but there's not enough to gain."
"You're right," he says, "and honestly, I'm actually more hurt
and deeply disappointed she would treat me worse than dirt."

She gently puts her hand on his and feels a tingling thrill.
I wonder just how long it's been since I felt that with Bill.
Apparently, he feels it, too; decides to take a shot:
"Revenge, you know, is what they call a dish that's
best served *hot.*"

"I think we've waited long enough." She winks and stands to go.
"And that will open two more spots. We ought to
let them know."
Now hand-in-hand, they saunter to the clerk and wait their turn,
both clueless of the bombshell which they are about to learn.

"Your name?" the clerk inquires. "It is Nelson," she replies.
"And Andrea's my first name." Her new friend has widened eyes.
"I bet you go by Andy," he presumes. "Well, yes, I do."
He laughs out loud and sputters, "It's just too good to be true."

"What's funny?" she's insisting, but the words just will not come.
He hands across his license with no pretense of aplomb.
"YOUR name is Andrew Nelson?" she says, gob-smacked
and aghast.
"I'm sure you go by Andy. This is gonna be a blast."

Once belly laughs subsided and they had a chance to think
they said goodbye to City Hall and went to get a drink.
But she had just one question, being smitten
through and through:
"Do you think as of right now that your nickname
could be Drew?"

~ The Prompt ~

Category:
Rhyming Short Story

Genre:
Rom Com

Theme:
Duplicate

Emotion:
Disappointment

Omi and Her Pigeons

I see the telltale flash of pink and gentle drop of the lace panel as I park in front of the brick bungalow. I'm on time, but I know my grandmother has been waiting for twenty minutes, and I hurry to reach her before she attempts to navigate the railing-free stairs alone.

"Hi, Omi," I say, strategically enveloping all five pudgy feet of her so as not to disturb her neon babushka.

You and the Queen, Omi. No one will miss you in a crowd.

She hugs back with an old-country ferocity that belies her eighty-seven years.

"Good morning, my Greta. We have a beautiful day for our errands."

My mother, Hildegard, was Omi's only child. After cancer stole Mom from both of us, I took over the weekly date.

Some Thursdays we toddle down Lincoln Avenue to authentic German shops: Dinkel's Bakery, Merz Apothecary, Salamander Shoes. Sometimes it's a trip to the doctor or dentist. No matter what, by mid-afternoon we are on our bench in Theodore Gross Park. This ritual is sacrosanct.

"What's today's treat, Omi?" I ask. She produces an ancient yellow Tupperware from within a prehistoric canvas tote.

"Zimtsterne." One bite of the hazelnut-almond cookie transports me to my mother's kitchen.

A woman pulls a red wagon miraculously keeping two rambunctious toddlers corralled, part of a steady stream of pedestrians, bikes, and strollers. It's a masterclass in pressing flowers, the flattened pink and white cherry blossoms now sidewalk tattoos.

The park's resident pigeons are oblivious to the bustle, pecking for tidbits only they can see.

"Do you know what the pigeons make me think of, Hildegard?"

Oh, Omi. You used to just repeat the story. Now you're calling me the wrong name.

"What's that, Omi?"

"The war, Meine Schatzi. Thousands of carrier pigeons flew from the battlefield with messages for officers tied to their tiny legs. You never hear of this, Hildegard?"

"That does sound familiar." I take another cookie. A couple kids are struggling to get on the seesaw. *The smaller one needs to get on first, you guys. C'mon. You can figure it out.*

"Of course, some messages were too important for birds. That's where I came in. I was one of the top agents during the war."

What did she just say?

"You were a secret agent during World War Two?"

"Oh, yes. Did I never tell you that? I told Hildegard…" Omi examines my face. "But you are not Hildegard; you are Greta, ja?"

"That's right, Omi. I'm Greta."

Reassured, she continues.

"Young women in Germany were nearly invisible in those days."

Not much has changed, Omi, even in America.

"Not the Jews, of course, but other girls could come and go as they pleased. I was on the country road, and a U.S. soldier came out of the field. He was no older than me and just as scared. He was part of a secret group that had been watching me, and knew my comings and goings would raise no suspicion.

"The plan was I would work for the Nazis and then give the information to him. It took much convincing, but I knew what was important and finally agreed. His name was Harold McKenzie and was from right here in Chicago. That's part of what brought me here after the war."

"That's amazing, Omi," I say. "You'll have to tell me more about it on our next visit."

***

I sit at the curb, but the lace curtain remains still, just as it did two Thursdays ago when I found Omi. What I'd give for one more talk on our bench. I've dreaded this task, but I owe it to Mom *and* Omi to see it through.

Later, my back aches from packing and my heart aches from reliving times and people I will never encounter again. I think I'm done, but find another box shoved far under Omi's bed.

I raise the lid, labeled ***Meine Ehre heißt Treue*** (translation: My Honor is Loyalty).

An Omi I never knew is inside.

A swastika-emblazoned frame surrounds a young, proud Margrete Schmitt—my namesake—smiling broadly with Heinrich Himmler. A letter of commendation is beneath it, honoring Omi for her success in deceiving the Allies. The further I dive in, the more my stomach turns. When I see the Trib obit for fallen war hero Harold McKenzie—killed in a covert operation gone wrong—I close the box.

Yes, my Omi was a double agent for the Nazis.

I just never imagined the last victim of her deception would be me.

~ The Prompt ~

Category:
Flash Fiction

Story must touch on this paragraph in some way:

The cherry blossoms floated gently down, landing on their blanket. They had just started eating when a pigeon landed by their basket. They both stared wide-eyed as the bird walked closer, unafraid.
Then they noticed a tiny scroll of paper attached to its right leg...

The Little Woman

If AARP ever decides to get into the Cirque Du Soleil game, I'm their gal. I was in the middle of my signature contortion—raising the nine-inch zipper on the back of my beaded gown—when Gerald walked into the bedroom. Single-minded and oblivious to my huffing and puffing, he retrieved a handkerchief from his bureau, turned on his heel, and exited as quickly as he'd entered. His "Almost ready?" grunt on the way out was the only sign he'd even noticed I was there.

It didn't faze me anymore. After forty years, what is there to do but grunt?

It wasn't always this way.

We were college seniors when a friend forced us on a blind date. I was an Eastern European History and Literature major, and he was in some new science program about things like bite marks, fingerprinting, and other crime scene niceties. It was a ridiculous idea.

What would I say at dinner? "Gee, what kind of blood splatter pattern do you think was left on the palace walls when the Romanovs were assassinated?"

Nevertheless, we clicked. We married right after graduation. Gerald got a job with a local police department and I got pregnant.

My career could wait. Not a big call for experts on dead communist authors in those days anyway.

When DNA testing became a reality in the mid-80s, Gerald Lane became a hot commodity. He had kept up on advances—including DNA—in forensics and was a slam dunk when he applied for the FBI Lab at Quantico.

With two toddlers and me pregnant again, it was a long drive from Des Moines to our new home in Warrenton, Virginia. We stopped about halfway to spend the night at a Motel 6. After a swim, the girls conked out, and Gerald and I lay awake in the double bed, his hand on my belly, sharing dreams and plans as if we were newlyweds again.

Though it would be four months before what would become our last baby—another girl—was born, we fantasized much further into our future.

For Gerald, the FBI Lab was just the beginning, a place to prove himself. Scientific breakthroughs, innovations, new methodology, cold cases solved. He would be a legend in his own time, constantly promoted until he achieved his ultimate dream: once he'd done all he could for the FBI—all he could do domestically, the CIA would come calling so he could work his magic there and make a difference on a global stage.

And me? I hadn't forgotten my own dreams and aspirations. It would take a little longer, but everyone knows time flies. Once the girls were in school, my own career would explode onto the scene. The capital was filled with history and culture—museums, libraries, universities, societies. Soon, Washington, D.C. would be my proverbial oyster.

Everything was great at first. Gerald put his plan into action and saw immediate results. His career seemed to be in a race with our girls to see who could grow the fastest. Before we knew it, our youngest was finishing high school and Gerald was shaking hands with his new boss, the Director of the CIA.

My own dream? It kept getting deferred. In those days (remember, this was over twenty years ago), if you were the wife of a government big shot, his job came first. There were social events, meet and greets, and dinners with other government officials who were even bigger shots. They all became the first and most important things in both of our date books.

So, wives' luncheons and committees and fundraising galas filled the void where my career was supposed to be. Want to know a little secret? It wasn't so bad. I had plenty of time, and I figured even if I was 75 before I got a job at the museum, all the stuff inside would still be a lot older than me. Life was good.

Let me rephrase that. Public life was good. My private life was in shambles.

It's a terrible thing when someone believes their own press. Gerald—just as he had planned—was proclaimed a wunderkind of forensic science. God's gift (had scientists believed in God) to criminology, justice, homeland security, and the future of forensics.

Gerald didn't think he was God's gift to anyone or anything. Gerald thought he *was* God.

Of course, legend tells us that even the real God needed help from "the little woman" [see also: "Mary, The Virgin"]. It was the same for Gerald. But the smiling, convivial, arm-in-arm couple at public events had become all but strangers at home. Was this "arrangement" so different than so many other couples found in politics, big business, and even royalty?

That notwithstanding, I began to feel trapped in a lonely, depressing isolation. I assumed Gerald had just grown weary of his aging, slightly pudgy wife. But when the late nights at the office became increasingly frequent, I suspected it was more than that. How much longer could I put myself though this public façade and inner turmoil?

The answer came one day in, of all places, the laundry room.

I never had sons, but laundry day gave me a glimpse into that dynamic. That was when I had to unroll balled-up socks, turn down the cuffs on sleeves, and search every pocket lest something vile go through the wash and ruin the whole load. Although I was spared the indignity of mud balls, worms, and other young boy unpleasantries, I've confiscated my share of change, pens, Kleenex, paper clips, business cards and, on a particularly profitable day, a one-hundred-dollar bill. Finders keepers, you know.

Then came the day I hit the jackpot.

I reached into the front pants pocket at usual, but my hand got stuck partway in. Did you know there's a tiny, flat pocket within the big pocket? I didn't. I looked it up—it's a holdover from the old days when men carried pocket watches. I'm guessing Gerald never knew it was there either, because that's where I found the errant slip of paper with the phone number.

It wasn't Gerald's writing—was it a woman's? Looked like the torn corner of napkin. She probably used the other part to blot her lipstick. Bitch.

I had to call the number, but I'd read enough mystery novels to know not to use my own phone. I decided to go full-on Agatha Christie. I donned a scarf and dark glasses, grabbed cash from the safe, and hailed a cab. Uber records could be traced, you know.

I chose an ethnic, middle-class neighborhood in the District and asked the cabbie to wait while I ran into the phone store. Less than an hour later I flipped open my new burner phone.

My hand shook as I punched in the number from the napkin. Instead of the breathy voice of Gerald's mistress, a message greeted me… or rather, greeted Gerald, by name. With instructions on where and who to meet with the classified information. Even thirty years later I knew a Russian accent when I heard one.

I went looking for infidelity. I found espionage.

This shocking turn of events got me thinking. All these years of Gerald's alienation. The heartache. The desolation. What I needed was a hobby! I'd heard good things about photography, so I started with that.

Nowadays, you don't even need a camera to be a good photographer. I upgraded to a burner smartphone and was good to go.

It's funny. My husband, the master of analyzing data, of sending criminals to their death over a stray eyelash, had no idea I was following him. I guess if someone has become invisible to you, that carries over outside the home as well.

Even if Gerald didn't see me, the press or the public might. I went to local coffeehouses and used public Wi-Fi and my new, unregistered tablet, to research the locations of the meetings. I became a master of disguise and blending into the crowd. The paparazzi would have found Waldo long before they would have found me.

As much fun as playing detective was, something was missing. It would be so much more interesting if, in addition to the pictures, I knew *what* classified information he was leaking. I suppose I could have tried that "As Seen on TV" distance listening device, but I didn't have to go to all that trouble.

It had been a long time since Gerald remembered or acknowledged that I had a brain. That worked to my advantage when I tried to get into his personal computer. Third time the charm on my password attempt: LaneforPrez2032. I wouldn't start printing the bumper stickers just yet, Gerald.

Even I couldn't believe his stupidity. No, it wasn't really that. It was arrogance. The future President Lane was never going to be caught. I could almost hear him thinking, "This is my *personal* computer. The government will never see this." Sheesh.

I copied the files onto a flash drive and shut down the computer. Nothing to do now but wait.

"Shirley, the limo is here."

The bark from downstairs snapped me back to the present. I took a last look at my hair, grabbed my evening bag, and switched off the light.

We sat facing each other in the limo. Although the pretense of small talk had been abandoned years earlier, I felt the need to say something.

"It's going to be quite a night," I said. Little did he know.

"Yeah," he said. Another trademark grunt.

I thought about saying more but decided to save my breath. I knew I'd have a lot of talking to do later and wanted to be fully ready.

As usual, Gerald was on his phone. I reached into my bag, being sure to take out the burner. I confirmed the text was ready to go.

Twenty-four hours earlier, I used the burner to send all the evidence I'd collected over the years to the Attorney General and Directors of Homeland Security, FBI, and CIA, along with the following message:

> *The attached file contains electronic and photographic evidence of treasonous acts committed by Gerald Lane, Director of Forensics for the Central Intelligence Agency. The evidence shows Lane providing classified information to multiple Russian agents. Lane will be the guest of honor at the National Union Building on Saturday, August 17, 2024, in celebration of his retirement. Just prior to that event tomorrow, I will send this message to The Washington Post, but without the attached files. If Lane is not publicly taken into custody at that event, I will follow up with The Washington Post and include the files.*

We turned a corner and the venue came into view. I sent the message to the Post and returned the phone to my bag.

Gerald was in his glory. The potential for election year pandering had brought out even more people than he'd expected. I smiled politely at people I'd never have to see again after tonight and sipped my white wine. I doubted they would make their move during the cocktail hour, with hundreds of people scattered throughout the atrium. They would wait until everyone was seated in the ballroom, Gerald front and center.

The loudspeaker crackled, and an elegant voice gently invited guests to make their way to the ballroom and be seated for dinner. A decent husband would have come to find me, but Gerald was too busy preening to think of that. I hung back, and when a helpful staff member invited me personally to go in, I effected a demure and slightly embarrassed posture and said I'd better run to the ladies' room before the program.

As expected, it was empty. I had gone through the entire historic building the week before, ostensibly to assist with final details about decorations and the like. In fact, I needed to be sure that the ladies' room, in a bid toward historic authenticity, was outfitted with toilets that still used a lidded tank. It was.

I entered the handicapped stall and closed the door. I took out the burner phone, removed the battery and SIM card, and flushed them. I removed the lid. A plastic bag was attached to the underside with duct tape. I removed the bag, inserted the phone, reused the tape to affix the phone to the inside of the tank away from the mechanism, and replaced the lid. My associate would retrieve it later.

I opened the bag and took out a small piece of flimsy paper…looked like the corner torn off a napkin. It displayed a single phone number. I committed it to memory and flushed the paper. Time to join the party.

The next few days were a blur. We made it through the salad course, but the Feds got to our table before the rubber chicken. The Post photographer did a great job of capturing my shock and disbelief, and my acting must be every bit as good as my talents at disguise, because I was interrogated for hours and they are convinced I didn't know a thing.

Even better, all those photo ops with Gerald are really paying off now. I'm America's sweetheart, having been duped by a charming double agent. The faithful housewife, who gave up her own career for him. Now what will she do? I wouldn't be surprised if there's a Netflix series and a GoFundMe page in my future.

But don't worry about me. It took forty years, but I finally have a job of my own. I'm putting all my new skills to use. Best of all, I'm finally using my major. Amazing how fast a language comes back to you.

Oh, gotta go. That's my new burner phone. Probably the boss.

"*Privet.* Yes, good morning, Minister. I'm ready for my next assignment."

~ The Prompt ~

Category: Short story

Genre: Spy

Subject: Loneliness

Character: Forensics Expert

Playing for Keeps

For Peggy and Vince, love had always been a sure thing.
Would that luck continue in the High Roller Lounge?

Peggy leaned her cane against the side of the slot machine and settled into the luxurious seat.

"Can you believe it, Vince? All these years and finally—the high roller room! I mean, they don't call it that. I guess that would be tacky. It's the 'VIP Lounge.' That's what it says over the door. I've never been a VIP anywhere. Well, maybe that one time we went to the auto show when you worked at the dealership and we got to go early. Was that a VIP thing? I don't remember. It was so long ago. Anyway, we are VIPs today. And I sure feel like one."

She surveyed the room.

"Oh good. We aren't the only ones. I didn't want to be the only ones, especially in the high roll—I mean, VIP lounge."

Peggy reached into her purse and brought out two classic troll dolls. She plucked an errant piece of Kleenex from a shock of glittery bright pink hair and placed the doll atop her slot machine. The other, sporting an emerald green mane that needed no further touch-up, went to his usual place of honor atop Vince's machine. Their bug-eyed expressions and disheveled, Albert Einstein-esque tresses gave the impression they enjoyed sticking forks into electrical outlets in their spare time.

"Welcome to the VIP lounge, Lady Luck and Mr. Big. I never thought we'd make it here, did you?"

It was the very definition of a rhetorical question, and not just because the dolls were made of plastic and nylon fiber. When Peggy was talking—whether making statements or asking questions—even the casino's most skilled oddsmakers wouldn't take the bet that someone could get a word in edgewise. Honestly, you'd be hard pressed to find anyone who had heard a peep out of Vince in years.

"Remember when we first started going to the gambling boat, Vince? We had to drive two and a half hours to Davenport to the boat on the Mississippi. We both hated that big bridge that crossed from Illinois to Iowa, so we found that small one. The big one was probably safer, but we didn't care.

"We loved the boat right away. Maybe too much, if I'm honest. But it was like the good old days when we'd play poker with our friends when the kids were little. If we won big, we had grocery money—probably someone else's grocery money. Those were tough times. They never really got much easier, did they? I guess that's why we wanted to dream big on the boat."

She turned her attention back to Lady Luck and Mr. Big.

"Our granddaughter was sure you would bring us luck. Christmas of—what was it, Vince, 1995 or '96? You always remember dates better than me. Well, it was the year Rachel was eleven, I think. I'm not sure she was supposed to know Grandma and Grandpa's 'hobby,' but she did, and she read that trolls were lucky—that girl read everything she could get her hands on—so, she found the two perfect ones to bring us luck. You've done alright by us, too.

"Vince. Remember that big jackpot we won the next spring? By that time there were boats on the Fox River, so our 'hobby' got more frequent. We were playing that Red White and Blue Sevens machine on the corner seat. They're right about the corner machines being luckier. We proved that. Well, I was putting in quarter tokens, and when I got the Red White and Blue I almost wet my pants! Of course, it was also because I should have gotten up long before I won, but you know the rules—you don't leave a hot machine. What a night! I still have one of the winning tokens. I've kept it for good luck."

Peggy took a breath and looked around the VIP lounge.

"It sure seems like there are a lot more winners in here than in the regular part of the casino. You always said, Vince, only the high rollers really win. I have a good feeling that today's our turn. I know, I know. I've made that prediction before but something tells me today is different.

"And you know, even if we don't get lucky in here, there's so much to do at this resort. There's that big Legends Tribute Theatre next to the main casino. We missed the Elvis show last week, but this weekend there's a Frank Sinatra and Judy Garland show. Wouldn't that be great to see?

"Oh! Remember when we saw Frank Sinatra at the Stadium in Chicago, Vince? What a night. The wife of the guy you worked with, I can't remember her name, but she *loved* Frank Sinatra since she was a bobby soxer. Norm got that big van and we all drove together, and she thought we were going to the circus. We went on and on about the circus, and how excited we were. The we turned the corner and she saw the marquee: 'One Night Only – Frank Sinatra.' She started screaming, 'Oh, you wonderful man!' and was hugging her husband. Then she said, 'I wondered why all of you were so excited about the stupid circus.' It was great. They were a nice couple."

Peggy went back to scanning the lounge and caught her reflection in a mirror and furrowed her already wrinkled brow.

"Sometimes I feel like everyone I see is getting younger and younger and I'm staying old. Do you ever feel that way Vince? And Lady Luck," she added as she ran a hand through her unruly gray hair, "when did we start going to the same hairdresser?"

Peggy let out the unbridled laugh reserved for family and friends and turned back to the slot machine.

"One of the great things about you, Vince, is you've always seen me as that twenty-five-year-old you met in 1954. We were quite a couple, if I do say so myself. Speaking of Judy Garland, everyone thought I looked like her. And I did.

"And you! I don't know who I'd compare you to. Rock Hudson? Cary Grant? Tall, dark, and handsome. Look that up in the encyclopedia and it says 'Peggy's Vince' right next to it. Come to think of it, I guess I still see you as a twenty-five-year-old, too.

"Maybe that's what got us through the hard times. There weren't too many years where we weren't worried about that grocery money every week. Or new shoes for the kids, or whether you'd sell enough cars so we could pay the mortgage. But we got by, somehow. And there were always things to celebrate.

"Our four great kids. Yeah, we wanted to kill them at times—especially those nights you were working late at the dealership, and it was just me trying to corral them. But thank God we let them live so they could give us our grandchildren. Right, Vince? Remember what you said when Rachel was born and Mike brought you over a cigar? 'Best cigar I ever smoked.' And you meant it.

"And that trip to Las Vegas! Remember that? You were working for that tiny used car lot then. The owner was a pill, but every once in a while, he'd surprise us and do something nice. He gave us a used car one year when we needed one and couldn't even afford to buy one from him at cost. Of course, we couldn't afford it because he was a cheapskate. But the trip; the trip was the best.

"He knew we loved the boat, so he gave you a trip to Vegas as a bonus. Funny, Vince, how you would never fly anywhere, but a free to trip to Vegas and it was up, up and away! That was really the only vacation the two of us ever took in our whole marriage, other than the few days we had for a honeymoon before our money ran out and we had to drive back to Chicago. We even managed to leave the casino and see Hoover Dam one day. It seems like a million years ago, and yet I remember it like it was yesterday."

Bells went off in the next row over, and a woman screamed "Jackpot!" as coins poured out of her machine.

"That's another thing I love about this casino, Vince. It still has real slot machines with real tokens. Remember when they brought in video machines and switched to credits? That's not for me. I want to put something in the machine, pull the handle, and watch the reels spin. You can do that here.

"Of course, even here they don't let you smoke inside anymore. Oh, smoking. Those were the days. I loved smoking. Maybe—no, definitely—too much, if I'm honest. And even though you never smoked, you understood. If you were coming home from work late, you'd stop and bring me a pack of cigarettes and a candy bar—a Maple Bun, if they had it. Do you know how many people I've told that story to, Vince? You're a hero to all of them, even the ones that never smoked.

"How long since I quit smoking, Vince? I really don't remember. All I know is it wasn't soon enough."

There was a rare break in Peggy's monologue as she relived those days.

"When I got sick, you took such good care of me, Vince. I so wanted to come home from the nursing home, and you made it happen. You arranged for the oxygen and the hospital bed; you helped me onto the commode and emptied it without complaint. You allowed me to spend my last months in the home that I loved."

Peggy summoned a casino worker.

"Can you please tell me the current day and time on Earth, United States of America, State of Illinois?"

She was elated to hear his answer and reached in her purse for the bright red lipstick Vince had always loved. As she applied it, a young woman asked if the empty seat next to her was taken.

Peggy beamed and said, "No dear, I'm sorry. That's my husband's seat. He's arriving any minute."

Chimes rang out over the loudspeaker, indicating the arrival of a new guest to the Shangri-La Casino and Resort. Peggy turned to the doorway where the gatekeeper, Peter, was unfurling an ancient scroll. Seated before him in a wheelchair was a frail and confused-looking elderly man. It took two tries, but he finally heard Peter's question and confirmed he was the person listed on the scroll. Peter made a sweeping motion to invite him in.

Peggy stood up and watched as the attendant rolled Vince over the threshold into the VIP Lounge. She instinctively grabbed her cane, but realized at once she no longer needed it. The instant their eyes met, an amazing transformation began for Peggy and Vince.

Vince all but leapt out of the wheelchair, his legs strong and steady and his mind clear. They watched in amazement as each other's wrinkles softened, joints stopped aching, spare tires and double chins vanished, and hair returned to a dark brown luster.

Peggy tossed her cane aside and, for the first time in decades, she and Vince ran toward each other. She jumped into his arms, once again a beautiful and vivacious twenty-five-year-old being swung in the air by her handsome movie star husband. All that was missing was the cigarettes.

In a moment reminiscent of the iconic Times Square photo at the end of World War II, Peggy's newly flexible body was bent backward in a kiss to make up for so much lost time. She then silently took Vince's hand and led him back to their machines.

"Mr. Big has been saving your seat for twelve years, Vince, and so have I." Vince mimed brushing twelve years of dust from the chair, and sat down with a flourish.

They sat holding hands and gazing at each other for a long time. Peggy finally broke the silence.

"I just don't know what to say."

"Well, that's a first," Vince said, smirking.

"You haven't changed a bit," Peggy replied. "Now, don't you think we should try this high roller—I mean VIP—Lounge before they kick us out?"

She handed Vince a tub of tokens before picking up her own.

"Oh, wait!" she said. "Don't start. I have something for you."

She delved into the bowels of her purse and dug around for a few minutes.

"Got it!"

She handed over a token, it's stamping worn, but still readable: Hollywood Casino – Aurora, Illinois on one side; twenty-five cents – Not Legal Tender on the other. Vince looked puzzled.

"Don't you remember? Our first big win after we got Lady Luck and Mr. Big? The Red White and Blue Sevens machine? We won $2,500! It was like winning a million for us. This is one of the tokens. My lucky token. I've saved it all these years."

"Well then, are you sure you want me to use it? Don't you want to hang onto it?"

Peggy leaned over, kissed Vince, and gently rubbed his cheek.

"I don't need a good luck charm anymore, Vince. It's done its job."

Peggy settled back into her VIP Lounge seat. She and Vince exchanged a knowing glance, then reached up and rubbed the heads of Lady Luck and Mr. Big, respectively.

"Three, two, one," Peggy said, and they pulled the arms on their slot machines in unison.

~ The Prompt ~

Category:
Short Story

Setting:
Casino

Character:
Troll

Must include:
A physical scroll

Fairy Godmothers:
"Solving Problems is Like Riding a Bike"

Once upon a time there was a girl who had a wicked stepmother. And, thanks to that girl, lots of other girls have a better chance of living happily ever after.

Lucy set the broken chain down and wiped grease onto her apron. It was after hours in her father's bicycle shop, and she could tinker to her heart's content. Before her mother's death two years ago, she was always in the shop. But her father's new wife—Lucy was loathe to call her a stepmother—was firmly rooted in the decorum of the Victorian age, even in 1895 Brooklyn, USA. She was determined to transform fifteen-year-old Lucy into a proper society lady, despite the negligence of the girl's mortifyingly common mother. Step one was to ban her from the crude bicycle shop.

Gas fixtures cast a calming glow through the room and illuminated the placard that invited customers to "Sell Your Horse and Buy a Bicycle." Her uncomfortable, billowing skirt had been carefully draped on a chair under the sign, both to keep it free from telltale grease, and to allow her to enjoy the trousers she secretly wore underneath.

Oh, for that wonderful day Mother and I wore bloomers in Central Park!

Her reticule was beside the skirt and Lucy pulled the dog-eared newspaper clipping and tintype from the small drawstring bag.

Along with the sunflower brooch she always wore, these keepsakes memorialized the strong, forward-thinking woman her mother had been, marching for women's rights at the polling place, in the workforce, and beyond. The newspaperman had tried to shame her for bringing a child to the rally, but her mother held her ground and had been quoted in print. "If we have each generation wait until they are grown, pray tell when, sir, will equality ever be achieved?"

Pray tell when, indeed. First, grief, and then the charms of his new wife have made Father forget his support of women's suffrage and Mother's other causes. I have also become invisible to him. How shall I continue Mother's good work when I am denied an education and career in favor of table manners and other such poppycock?

Something flashed behind Lucy. She spun and saw a blinding column of light streaming from a broken bicycle mirror. When the room came into focus, a short, elderly woman in a black robe stood before Lucy.

"Good evening, Lucy. It would seem, pray tell, that the time is now."

Lucky was dumbstruck. She had seen Kellar the Magician at the Herald Square Theatre, but even he hadn't performed such an illusion.

"Don't be afraid, Lucy. I'm here to help you."

"Who are you? Where did you come from?"

"I'm a friend from far in the future—more than a hundred years." The woman sighed. "I'm sorry to report that, even a century hence, women's battle for equality still rages. But, thanks to the work of people like your fine mother, advances have been made."

"How do you know of my mother's work?" Lucy asked.

"I've spoken to her about it."

"You mean you're—"

"Yes, I'm afraid I had to leave my earthly bounds before all of my work there was done too," the woman said. "But enough about my past. I'm here to help you with the present."

She sat down next to Lucy and waved her hand in front of them. A large rectangle of light hung in the air, and images quickly filled the virtual frame.

"What… how?"

"Don't worry, my dear. I'm borrowing a bit of twenty-first century technology to give you a peek into your not-so-distant future. I think you'll be pleased with what you see."

The magical show began; Lucy was transfixed. At first, newspaper images filled the area as if invisible hands were swapping one broadsheet for the next. But then, people—first in the sepia tone of the tintype and then in full color—moved about the area as if another, Lilliputian world had materialized in the small space! It was a Jules Verne novel come to life in the repair room of the Burns Bicycle Emporium.

But it was not the science fiction histrionics that touched Lucy to her core. It was the content. The moving pictures ended; the woman continued.

"You are destined, Lucy, to be a critical link in the chain of people who have and will work tirelessly for women's—and human—rights. Your name is already written in the history books. There are a hundred years of men and women between us that were able to do what they did because of your actions now, and throughout the rest of your life."

"But what of my father's wife? She is determined to keep me in my place."

The woman laughed. "She, and many others through the ages. Her misplaced priorities will soon leave her no time to worry about you. She is no match for your passion and purpose.

"However, when you do come upon obstacles, and you surely will, there are two things to give you power and strength."

She reached out and touched the sunflower brooch.

"You carry the spirit of your mother in this talisman she left behind. She is with you whenever you wear it."

"And the other?"

The woman reached behind her neck and undid a clasp. "And this will give you strength when you need it." She fastened her silver, bejeweled, armor-shaped collar around Lucy's neck.

"It's time for me to go. There are many others struggling on their journey whom I need to visit."

"Wait!" Lucy pleaded, grabbing the woman's sleeve.

"You have all the tools you need. Trust yourself."

Lucy released her hold.

"How can I thank you? I don't even know your name."

"My name is Ruth." She winked. "But my friends call me RBG." Another flash, and she was gone.

Lucy removed her apron, grabbed her bag, and went out the front door, leaving her Victorian skirt behind.

And she lived notoriously ever after.

~ The Prompt ~

Category:
Flash Fiction

Genre:
Fairy Tale

Location:
A bike repair shop

Object:
A broken mirror

Individual Results May Vary

Arthur thought anything was better than going through life fat and alone. That is, until an experimental weight-loss program left him with more than just a bad taste in his mouth.

For the third time in as many hours, Arthur thought about killing Eve. Not whether to do it; that decision was made long ago. What he thought about these days was how. There was only a slim chance of killing her and living to tell about it, but on a day like this, nearly any consequence was worth the thought of just shutting her up.

"You can't eat that," Eve shrieked as Arthur reached for a cracker. "You're already over your carb limit for the day. How many times do I have to tell you the same thing? Do you want to get fat again? How selfish can you be?"

On and on she droned, the same broken record that began playing the day they came home from the treatment center, and on a constant loop ever since.

Yeah, I'd love to be fat again. Arthur reached for a goddamn celery stick. *Because when I was fat, I was alone.*

Alone. The very thought transformed the celery into double chocolate cheesecake.

Having temporarily silenced Eve with an acceptable snack choice, Arthur reveled in the silence and let his mind wander back to the day that changed his life forever.

One year ago, 2057. Technology had advanced to a realm that made science fiction writers look like historians. Every day brought new advances in science and medicine; people now associated the word extinct with diseases, not animals. But one chronic condition stumped the doctors and refused to be eradicated.

Americans were still fat. No, not fat. Obese.

And while 200-plus was the new thin, that weight was a spec in Arthur's rear view mirror. At 500-plus pounds and counting, Arthur was grossly obese. Morbidly obese, according to his doctor.

Just like every fat person, he had his story of how he got to this point. Through college, he was in great shape; an athlete who scored regularly, on and off the field. That is, until his senior year, when Arthur met Joan. Chemistry turned to passion in an instant, and they planned to combine their graduation party with a wedding reception.

All that changed as Arthur stood at the front of the campus chapel, waiting for a bride who never came. He likely would have stood there forever, in a fog of embarrassment and confusion, if not for his best man, who not only led him away, but also invited the guests to stay for the reception anyway, because, well, what the hell, it was paid for and there was beer.

Arthur would tell anybody that would listen that he just pulled up a chair to the buffet that night and hadn't stopped eating since. A fantastic job and enormous salary only heightened all his appetites and made it easier for him to become a big man in every way.

Of course, that didn't mean that Arthur didn't want to lose weight. It had been years since a woman had shown any interest in him, and even a steady diet of hookers had proved unsatisfying.

So, he tried all the magic elixirs, the pills, the fad diets, the miracle creams. Each left him angrier, more desperate, and fatter.

Fast forward to a year ago. Arthur had long since sworn off the "cures," resigning himself to being fat and alone for the rest of his life. Then he saw the ad.

Surely, they couldn't really deliver on what they were promising. Alright, it was the second half of the twenty-first century—barely—but still. It was absurd. No person with half a brain would even consider it.

For the first time in years, Arthur felt hope. He read the ad again.

Are you morbidly obese? Are you alone? Let the doctors at the Meiosis Transformation Clinic solve both of your problems! Send a transmission today to apply to be part of our revolutionary program which will end obesity while providing companionship. You deserve to be happy. Come join us today.

Arthur asked few questions and eagerly signed on the dotted line when told he was an ideal candidate for the program. So what if it was an experimental study involving new surgery? What did he have to lose, except this goddamn weight?

And they promised he would also be leaving the facility with a woman! And not just any woman. They assured him that their scientific process would produce a match for him that was as close as humanly possible and guaranteed that she would go home with him without an argument. Arthur didn't care if they were going to pick her at random from a cargo hold full of broads bought on the open market—he was going home thin and with a woman. And it only took a week!

The day of the procedure came. Arthur had already wired the million dollars and showed up as instructed with just the fat clothes on his back. The clinic would provide his new wardrobe as part of its services, since none of his old clothes would fit anymore. After signing a thick stack of forms, he watched as a nurse put a needle in his arm and started the anesthetic.

"See you in a week," he remembers her saying as he drifted off.

"Why the hell did you buy two percent milk?"

Eve's condescending shout snapped Arthur out of his daydream.

"You were right there with me, Eve," he responded through clenched teeth. "If you wanted skim, why didn't you say something then?"

"You know I can't see what you're doing on that side," she snapped back. "That's probably how you snuck the cookies into the house, isn't it? You're trying to kill us both!"

"I don't know where this paranoia is coming from, Eve, but you must know that it's in my best interest to take care of both of us," Arthur replied. "Now, if you don't mind, I'd like to get something from the desk."

Eve grunted in response but nonetheless lifted herself up so that she and Arthur could walk across the room in unison, as they had done for the past year since emerging from the Meiosis Transformation Clinic as conjoined twins.

"What's so important you have to read it now?" she barked.

"The juicer isn't working right," Arthur replied as he rifled through the desk drawer. "I want to find the manual and the warranty. Here it is."

As Arthur angled to pull the manual out of the bottom drawer, several other papers fell to the floor, including a long-forgotten pamphlet. Arthur picked it up.

"You better get that juicer working right!" Eve shrieked. "We can't go without our healthy smoothies!"

"Don't worry, Eve, I will," he muttered automatically. "OK, I have what I need, we can sit down."

They clumsily plopped down on the couch and Eve grabbed the remote for the screen in the wall. As she became engrossed in the transmission, Arthur opened the pamphlet, and began reading:

MEIOSIS TRANSFORMATION CLINIC
PRECAUTIONS AFTER SURGERY

Under no circumstances should you consume any type of alcoholic beverages post-surgery. Because of the complexity of your procedure, this could cause an imbalance of the dual chemistry, likely resulting in the death, and eventual surgical removal, of your companion. Should you accidentally ingest alcohol, please report back to the clinic at once for emergency treatment.

Arthur looked up from the brochure and smiled at Eve.

"You know, Eve, it's been a year since we've been together," he said sweetly. "I think that calls for a drink."

~ The Prompt ~

Category:
Short Story

Genre:
Science Fiction

Theme:
Obesity

Character:
Conjoined Twin

Hidden in Plain Sight

Nearly fifty years later and this celebrity cold case remains unsolved. Yet the solution has been staring everyone in the face the whole time.

It takes a lot to shock teenagers these days. But a dead body in the classroom never disappoints.

I don't know if, technically, I'm a dead body. I'm a skeleton. My flesh rotted off these old bones almost fifty years ago, decomposing near a backyard pool in Las Vegas in 1975. So, how did I end up in a biology classroom at Lake Orion High School? Well, a truck brought me here (fitting, right?), but I'm getting ahead of myself. Let's go back to summer of '75.

I got sent away in '67 on trumped up charges. We had an arrangement that I'd still run the union from inside, but the key player welshed on that and sided with the Mob, so by the time Tricky Dick commuted my sentence five years later, I was back to square one.

By July of '75, my power grab had pissed off multiple Family members. It seemed a good thing when a couple of them suggested lunch, but we never got to the osso buco. I woke up in a trash bag in the trunk of a Caddy on a three-day trip to Vegas. I was DOA at the Don's hidden estate. One of the brainier goons knew a little sunbathing would have my meat "fallin' off da bone" fastest, so it was everybody out of the pool while I lay in state.

Afterward, they decided bones, dental records, and even ashes could still pose a problem. That's where they got creative, deciding a big man on campus like me should be on display in his hometown school.

Now normally, it's a complicated thing to pawn off a murder victim's skeleton on an unsuspecting public school. But don't forget about the power of unions. They don't call it a brotherhood for nothing.

A union trucker literally had a union teacher brother at Lake Orion. A union secretary easily fabricated a death certificate and official paperwork from a "Skeletons R Us" company and within a week I was hanging in this classroom.

Most kids freak out when they find out I'm not plastic. But not David. He's also a brainiac but has decided to use his powers for good instead of evil. He writes for something called the school website, and when he found out I was real, his reporter instinct kicked in. And since today is—holy shit—pretty much "The Jetsons" without the flying cars, it took David no time at all to disprove the paperwork and figure it all out.

That's why this straight-A, rule-abiding kid broke into school last night, and now has Jimmy Hoffa's pinky toe in his pocket, ready to send it off for something called DNA testing.

Not that proving things matters. Anybody who could be punished for killing me decomposed long ago too. Plus, truthfully, I probably had it coming.

I know my days here are numbered. Which is too bad.

I was really hoping to be around when David finds Amelia Earhart.

~ The Prompt ~

Category: Flash Fiction
Genre: Historical Fiction
Action: Forging a Document
Object: A Skeleton

Sisterhood of the Traveling Therianthropy

Like all abusers, Scott only showed his true colors at home. That's why it took a real chameleon to finally bring him down.

Scott dropped the free weights loudly onto the rack, knowing the flourish would attract the attention that fed his malignant narcissism. Roughly once a week he put on this show, as lifting was the only thing that worked to release the remaining adrenaline and calm him down enough to return home.

His sleeveless shirt wasn't called a wife beater for nothing.

Bridget stood at the kitchen sink and gingerly removed the ice pack from her cheek. The swelling wasn't too bad, but it would need a lot of makeup by morning.

Movement caught her eye. It was a chameleon on the window's outside sill, its front feet on the glass like a color-ambiguous Peeping Tom. They held each other's gaze for a few seconds before it disappeared from the sill.

Inexplicably captivated, Bridget walked out to the back yard to find it. After poking through the bushes under the window, she turned and yelped at the elderly woman standing in the yard.

"I didn't mean to startle you," the woman said, looking intently at Bridget's blackening eye. "Are you alright? Did someone hurt you?"

"Oh, no, I'm fine," she said, instinctively touching her face in a futile attempt to hide the bruise. "I just banged my face on the corner of the cabinet. What a klutz!"

Without being invited, the woman walked to a bench in the yard and sat down, drawing Bridget to her side like a magnet.

"I used to tell people I was a klutz," she said, pulling back the sleeve of her flowing blouse. A faded scar ran nearly the length of her forearm. "After a while, you start to believe it yourself."

Bridget unconsciously nodded. "How did you get free?"

"When you have the right friends, sometimes these matters take care of themselves."

Both women stood, and Bridget walked toward the house. She turned, and the woman was gone. Leaves fluttered as Bridget saw the chameleon's tail slip under the bushes.

It was never good when Scott came home this late. Nearly midnight meant it had been a full evening of booze-fueled paranoia. In the kitchen, Bridget heard the garage door.

He stumbled in, a madman.

"Where were you tonight?" he screamed, as if *she* had just come home.

"Right here," she pleaded, seeing no escape route.

"You didn't answer my text!" he bellowed.

"Yes, I did! Check your phone."

"Don't tell me what to do, you lying bitch!" Scott began throwing whatever he could reach. When he didn't connect, he lunged at her. She sank to the floor, and he began kicking. She bit her lip and remained silent, knowing her cries only prolonged the episode.

Eventually he stopped, physically tired and unfulfilled by her insufficient suffering. He'd make up for it next time.

"I'm going back to the gym. Get this mess cleaned up before I get back."

Bridget waited for the garage door to close. Clutching her battered side, she tentatively pulled herself up to the sink.

The chameleon was staring through the window.

Bridget crossed the kitchen and opened the back door. The woman was on the bench.

"You're the chameleon," she said, half statement, half question.

The woman gestured to the empty space beside her.

"But who? How…"

"I was once a prisoner of a monster like your husband. He abused me physically, mentally, and emotionally.

"We lived on a farm, and one day one of the stray cats transformed before my eyes into a woman. She was there to help, with one condition. Would I accept this special gift: the power to take whatever form necessary—human or animal—to help other women escape? I agreed.

"So, Bridget. Are you ready to accept the gift as well?"

At 1:00 a.m., there were only three cars in the lot of the 24-hour gym. Two men visible through the front windows were on rowing machines. A solitary hawk circled overhead, alighting near the side of the building.

Moments later, a chiseled bodybuilder came around the corner and through the front door.

"Weight room?" he grunted toward the two men. Both tilted their head toward a back hallway without even looking up.

Scott was deadlifting when the man came in. "Hey man," he said, turning on the charm reserved for strangers; desperate to impress the intimidating presence. "Welcome to insomniac lifting."

"I like it when it's not crowded," the man said. "But, hey, it's good to have a second so we can bench press. You interested?"

"Yeah," Scott answered, ready to show up the guy. "You want to go first?"

"Nah, you were here. Go for it. What do you bench? Two hundred, two-twenty?"

That was even a little much for Scott when cold sober, but he could never look weak. Never.

"I can do two-twenty in my sleep."

He racked the bar and laid on the bench. The man stood behind him to spot.

Scott took a deep breath and lifted the bar from the rack, then down to his chest. As he began to raise it up again, the man leaned over him, grabbing hold of the bar.

"Hey, man, what are you…" He trailed off as he watched the man's face transform—black eye and all—into that of his wife. He began to lose his grip on the bar, which was now above his throat.

"Good thing you had a spotter, huh Scott?" Bridget said. "Too bad I'm not strong enough to hold it either."

She let go and smiled as the bar crushed his windpipe, nearly decapitating him. It was quiet, except for the faint, rhythmic whirring of the machines in the other room. Bridget waited until she transformed back into the bodybuilder before giving Scott a swift kick for good measure. *In your sleep, huh? Well, nighty-night.*

The bodybuilder walked out of the gym unnoticed by the two guys, who likewise paid no attention to the beautiful hawk, gliding her way to freedom.

~ The Prompt ~

Category:
Flash Fiction

Genre:
Fantasy

Setting:
A weight room

Object:
A chameleon

A Mother's Work is Never Done

When grief has clouded a daughter's perception, only the mother she lost can help her see clearly again.

When I gave birth, your infant wails were music to my ears.
The night I died your anguished wails reduced the gods to tears.
The gates of heaven beckoned; angels ushered me away.
You begged me not to leave you, but I did not have a say.

It's true you stay a mother even when your kids grow old.
And now I know that even death does not release that hold.
It breaks my heart that grief still haunts you each and ev'ry day.
Now listen up, because your Mama has some things to say.

I first must tell you, darling, that my world is close to bliss
So any worries you possess I beg you to dismiss.
The loved ones who had gone before are answers to a prayer.
The only imperfection is to see you in despair.

I check on you quite regularly from my seat above.
God bless your friends who've showered you with
sympathy and love.
You've often told them I have sent a sign to all but you.
Your eyes are blind from grief because that simply is not true.

You even saw a charlatan—so many she misled—
With empty hopes and promises of contact with the dead.
To see or feel or hear me you don't need a magic wand.
For we are joined forever through our mother-daughter bond.

Do you recall that snowy day the car began to slide?
You barely missed the other car; were angels at your side?
Of course, you give them credit. That is natural to feel.
But how could you not know *I* turned the other driver's wheel?

You felt so sorry for yourself when Mike said he saw me
When visiting his mother as they shared a cup of tea.
She died just two weeks later, and I thought that you would know
I fortified the man you love to ease the coming blow.

And speaking of your husband, on the night you had that feud
All started by unfair remarks about your homemade food.
Remember as he slurped his soup—he really has no charm—
It all spilled down his shirt front…
don't you know who bumped his arm?

I thought it would be obvious as I performed these acts
The shorthand of our love would easily reveal the facts.
You only saw the outside; didn't feel me there with you.
And so, to ease your pain I knew the one thing I must do.

I come to you within your dreams to set the record straight
And beg forgiveness for the length of time you had to wait.
But now you'll know whenever there's an act of love you see
If it makes you feel better, you will know it came from me.

And if you still are questioning my twisty, zigzag route,
I guess I'll state the obvious; explain what it's about:
You needed no theatrics, special visions to be eyed.
Because, my love, as you should know, I've never left your side.

For now, I'll bid goodnight to my beloved whom I miss
And so that you'll remember on your brow I've placed a kiss.
I sense you have accepted that my promises I'll keep,
For as I steal a final look, you're smiling in your sleep.

~ The Prompt ~

Category:
Rhyming Short Story

Genre:
Ghost Story

Theme:
Never judge a book by its cover

Emotion:
Self-pity

Dead Men Tell No Tales

James set down the broken eyeglasses and switched on the gooseneck lamp. As always, his father's voice boomed in his head as he reached for the cabinet door.

"Calling all Rangers. This is Captain Video. I need your help."

Ready and waiting, Captain. The simple magnifying tool of his father's era had been replaced long ago by a state-of-the-art magnifying headset, complete with focus dial and LED lamps. The memory, however, hadn't changed.

***

In 1964, Chester Hamblin was still officially the "Son" of Hamblin & Son Funeral Home but was running the business alone after his father's stroke and subsequent move to a nursing home. That's when Chester—along with his wife, Helen, and three-year-old son—moved back into the mortuary's family living quarters where he had grown up.

It took a while for Helen to be comfortable with the unique living arrangement, but not Jimmy. On days with no viewings, he had free run of the main floor, thinking every house had a cool room filled with giant wooden boxes with lids and metal cookie jars up on pedestals. A feature article in the *Spring Valley Gazette* included a photo of a playful Jimmy peeking around the corner of a display casket, conjuring still-raw images of John John Kennedy under the Resolute Desk.

Jimmy was raised under the assumption he would ultimately take his rightful place in the Hamblin & Son organization. But Chester remembered the ham-fisted and scarring way his own father had introduced him to the business. ("What are you crying for, kid? It's just a dead body.") He was determined not to make the same mistakes with his own son.

On his eighth birthday, Jimmy was deemed old enough to go "downstairs," the mysterious, grown-ups-only place where the unseen work of the funeral home was done. As he stood in the middle of the large, bright room with his parents, Jimmy wondered what all the fuss had been about. With the tables and cabinets, it could have been anyone's workshop or garage, except for the three ominous white doors on the perimeter. He walked toward one of them.

"Sorry, Jimmy," his dad said, stepping next to him to block the door. "For now, you need to just stay in this part of the basement. Is that understood?"

"What's behind the doors?" Jimmy asked.

"That's where we help our friends get ready for their viewing and final services. I promise, one day you'll be able to go in there and watch me work and even help me someday. Just not yet."

Jimmy frowned. "What is there to do out here? It's boring."

"Boring!" Chester boomed. "Here in Captain Video's Secret Workshop?"

Jimmy had no idea who Captain Video was, but this sounded promising.

"This is where Captain Video uses his special powers and scientific equipment to save ancient artifacts."

He had Jimmy's full attention now.

Chester turned his back on Jimmy and opened a cabinet door. A moment later he turned with a flourish, sporting gigantic magnifying goggles and brandishing a soldering iron.

Jimmy's eyes were saucers.

"What Captain Video needs, Jimmy, is a Ranger to help him. Know anybody who could do that?"

"Me! Me!" he said, rushing to Chester.

"You seem like a fine candidate. But I need you to take the Captain Video Ranger oath. Will you do that?"

Jimmy raised his right hand without being prompted and shouted, "Yes!"

"Okay. Do you promise to answer when Captain Video calls for your help…"

"As long as your homework is done," Helen chimed in from upstairs.

Chester smiled. "Yes, as long as your homework is done. Do you promise?"

"I promise!"

"Do you promise to only use the special scientific tools when you have permission?"

"I promise!"

"Do you promise to *never* go into the rooms through the three doors until your father says it's okay?"

"I promise!"

"Alright then. You are officially a Captain Video Ranger, First Class. Congratulations, Ranger!"

Chester put out his hand and Jimmy shook it, unwittingly starting his transition from "son" to "& Son."

***

James carefully placed the eyeglasses into the clip to hold them steady. He used tweezers to pick up the broken end of one arm, dabbed each broken end with a bead of cyanoacrylate adhesive, and, with the steady hand and precision of a surgeon, rejoined the pieces and maintained his hold. It brought him back to his father's side.

Dad was fixing someone's broken glasses. The Captain Video thing was done by this time; I was probably thirteen or fourteen. I asked why we didn't just take another pair from the box in the basement; we always had shit like that hanging around. "It's not like he needs to see out of them," I said, laughing. He glared and told me to go upstairs. When I protested, he just said, "Upstairs, now." He didn't have to tell me again. When he came up later, he made me go into his office. I was terrified. He just stared at me for what seemed like ten minutes. Then he said, "The most important thing in this business is respect. I don't ever want to hear you joking about any of the deceased. Not even here. It is our job to show them respect. Do you understand?" All I could do was nod. "And the reason I am fixing Mr. Wilson's glasses instead of just replacing them is because you might not care or know the difference, but his family will. It will bring them comfort to see him looking as much like himself as possible. Now, go and think about all this, and when you're ready to approach things with the right attitude, you can help me again."

James gingerly released his hold and the arm of the glasses stayed together. He let out a breath he didn't know he was holding, removed the contraption from his head, and looked at the plaque above the table. "Dead Men Tell No Tales." He smiled and looked at his watch.

I better get going if I'm going to make that ribbon cutting on time. He glanced again at the plaque. *It's going to be good to see you, Eddie.*

Ed Kolar stood behind the half wall a step up from the settee area and gave the bowling alley a slow, 360-degree appraisal.

Take a good look, Dad. Are you thrilled or rolling in your grave? Well, I don't know if I've ever seen you thrilled, so I guess that's asking a lot. I just hope you're happy with the changes I made. Your name's still on the sign, so I hope I'm doing you proud.

Ed frowned.

Pride. It cost us a lot of years.

He walked over to the small serving bar and leaned in toward the pass-through window to the main bar. *Tens of thousands in renovations and they couldn't change this stupid thing.* "How's everything in there?"

"Ready to go, boss," a woman answered. "We're bringing the appetizers to the alley next."

"Great. Thanks." While still contorted over the bar, he grabbed the gun and expertly dispensed himself a Coke, a Cirque du Soleil move he perfected in high school. Of course, in those days, the move also included adding a shot of rum, but he needed to be sharp tonight.

"Everything looks great, Ed!" Chamber of Commerce Director Jennifer Walman was seeing the place for the first time. "I feel like a time traveler."

They met at the Chamber display table and shook hands.

"Imagine how I feel," Ed said, laughing. "I practically grew up in this place. It's a little Twilight Zone-ish for me."

"Everyone's going to love it, and we have a big crowd coming for the Grand Reopening ribbon cutting." She handed Ed a clipboard as evidence.

Although there were some newcomers, most of the list read like the Yellow Pages of his youth: Della's Flower Shoppe, Ted's Auto Body, The Snippery Hair Salon. Ed started.

Hamblin & Son Funeral Home.

Jimmy. I've been so wrapped up in the renovation. It didn't even occur to me that Jimmy would be here. All the times I've thought about him over the years, all the times I went to call or write, and then didn't. To explain why I left; why I didn't even say goodbye.

In a town like Spring Valley, it's hard to pinpoint the start of relationships, since pretty much everyone knew everyone else since birth. But Edward Kolar and James Hamblin knew the exact day they became best friends. Monday, October 30, 1967. The boys were in second grade and made the after-school discovery of the candy stash ready and waiting for the classroom party the next day.

In this, their first foray into juvenile delinquency, Ed and Jimmy boosted all the candy that would fit in their lunchboxes and then made the dubious decision (no Einsteins in the criminal game, you know) to get a head start on the holiday, meet after school, and eat all of it that night. When the crime was discovered in the morning, the classmates kept home from school with severe vomiting and diarrhea were the obvious suspects. Their parents got a confession—and a lot more—out of them with a threat of more candy.

They decided to give up their life of crime and became inseparable friends on the right side of the law: cub scouts, swim class, summer camp. Eddie—only Jimmy could call him that—was the only friend who had been brave enough to visit the Funeral Home basement and soon was duly sworn in as a Captain Video Ranger, one of only two in the whole town.

In turn, Jimmy was the only kid besides Eddie to get to go behind the scenes and see how the machine picked up the bowling pins and put them back in the right spots. It was like something on that outer space show his mom watched, *Star Trek*.

Their friendship grew as the boys did. They loved the freedom that working in a family business gave them, as well as the perks they shared with each other. Jimmy bowled (complete with surreptitious rum and Cokes) for free whenever he wanted to, and both boys talked cheerleaders into going to prom with them thanks to the promise of being squired in a real life limousine (sans hearse lead car).

By their junior year, Jimmy (with his parents' strong encouragement) had decided on Southern Illinois University, one of only five in the country that offered a degree in Mortuary Science. Eddie signed to bowl at Illinois State University, thanks to a full ride scholarship, majoring in Sports Administration.

Four years later, they were back home for good, they thought. James Hamblin, BMS, became a full partner with his father, but things didn't go so smoothly with Ed and his dad.

Louie Kolar was resistant to the "college boy" ideas Ed had brought home from school. "We've been doing fine for forty years; why change it now?" he'd say. Their arguments became more heated and more frequent.

Then came the fight that drove me away for good… or so I thought.

"Ed!" Jennifer said, elbowing his arm for added emphasis.

"Oh, sorry. What's up."

"I thought you'd like to say hello to *the Mayor*," she said, Hizzoner at her side. From her expression, Ed gathered it had taken several attempts to infiltrate his reverie.

"Mr. Mayor," Ed said, extending a hand. "It's an honor to have you here."

"Louie's Lanes has been a fixture in this town for half a century. I wouldn't miss this for the world."

"You're very kind, sir. And thank you for doing the honors at the ribbon cutting."

"Speaking of which," Jennifer said, "I think we're ready. Shall we go outside?"

Ed didn't know what was more dazzling when he walked outside: the 6:00 p.m. June sun or the throngs of people in attendance. He stood to the side behind the red ribbon as the mayor orated.

"Ladies and gentlemen. Louie's Lanes has been a fixture in this town for half a century. We all knew Louie and loved patronizing his business, no matter how lousy our bowling scores."

He waited for the compulsory polite laughter, then continued.

"When Louie became ill, his son, Edward, left his life behind in New York and came back to Spring Valley to be with his father at the end. And now, he not only continues his legacy, but has renovated Louie's Lanes for the new millennium. So, without further ado, welcome to the Grand Re-opening of Louie's Lanes!"

As the ribbon dropped, the double doors opened and people strode into the bright and colorful showplace. Ed hung back with Jennifer, smiling at the guests as they passed.

"Let's hope they like what they see," he said.

"It's just like in my business, Eddie."

Jimmy. He turned around.

"People are dying to get in there," they said in unison.

Both laughed, started a handshake, and abandoned it for a hug.

"C'mon, I'll buy you a beer," Eddie said, putting an arm around Jimmy's shoulder.

Three hours and a thousand gutter balls later, Ed thanked Jennifer and walked her to the door as the caterers closed the doors on their vans and headed out as well. Marci peeked her head through the archaic opening from the bar.

"I'm heading out boss; need anything else?"

"No, Marci. Thanks for your help. Get some rest."

"OK. I'll lock the bar door behind me. Get some rest too. Our first league starts in two nights."

Ed shook his head. *What have I gotten myself into?*

He reached for his keys as a dark sedan pulled up to the overhang. It was Jimmy.

"Forget something?" Eddie said as he held the door.

"I never got that beer—."

"That's easy to fix—"

"—or an explanation of why you left town."

Eddie let out a deep sigh. "Let's sit down."

Jimmy sat at a high top and Eddie brought back two beers. Eddie took a drink and began.

"I owe you more than an explanation. I owe you an apology. You're my best friend, and I left town without telling you and without saying goodbye. Believe me, I wanted to. But I couldn't. It was too hard.

"You know that after we got back from school, my dad was a stubborn ass about making any changes to the bowling alley. The place was falling apart around him and he didn't care. He didn't want to hear my ideas or spend any money. We were fighting constantly."

"That's why you left?"

"No. That's what everyone thought, but that wasn't it."

Eddie stared down and picked at the label on his bottle.

"Once I went away to school, I realized something about myself. I'd suspected it for a long time, even in high school. Shit, I had the head cheerleader in the back of a limousine and didn't even try to feel her up. That should have told me everything I needed to know. But it was college that made me understand and accept who I was, who I am."

"You're gay."

Eddie raised his head and met Jimmy's gaze.

"Yes. And when I realized it back then, I was in the closet and didn't know how to come out. And the worst thing? I was in love with someone. Really, really in love with someone.

"Remember, this was the 80s, so gay pride was everywhere. I guess I got caught up in it. I finally got up the courage and decided to come out… to my father."

"I'm guessing," Jimmy said, "it didn't go quite like in the afterschool special?"

Eddie's laugh was sardonic.

"He told me I was dead to him. He took five thousand dollars out of the safe, threw it at me, and told me I had one day to get out. So, I did. There was this guy from school who'd moved to New York, so I called him and hopped on a plane. Next time I heard from my dad was when he called to say he was dying. I guess cancer makes you forget you hate gays."

Jimmy waited a beat before speaking.

"But why didn't you call or write or let me know where you were? And you didn't need to face your father alone. Why didn't you tell me? Why, Eddie?"

"I didn't tell you for the same reason I didn't write or call. I was doing everything I could to try to forget and especially to not hurt the person I loved."

Now Eddie paused.

"You. I was in love with you."

Jimmy buried his face in his hands and moaned, "No, no."

"I know it's a shock—"

Jimmy bolted up and walked around the table to Eddie, pulling him to his feet.

"—and you probably hate me for it, but I just—"

Jimmy took Eddie's face in both hands and kissed him with a passion that had been building since Halloween, 1967. Eddie's body responded instinctively, returning the kiss with equal intensity. After, they held each other in silence, neither wanting to, nor, eventually, knowing how to let go.

Eddie finally broke the silence.

"No, you hang up first."

Both laughed and reluctantly pulled apart, their eyes shining with tears.

"All those wasted years," Jimmy said. "How could we both be so stupid?"

"Well, you work with dead people all day and I've probably been hit on the head with bowling pins more times than I'd like to count, so I guess that explains a lot," Eddie said.

"Well, we finally figured it out, thank God. Plus, now, we don't have to worry about your father causing us any trouble," Jimmy said. "Like it says on that plaque you gave me, dead men tell no tales."

~ The Prompt ~

Category:
Short story

Character:
Mortician

Setting:
Bowling alley

Must include:
Broken eyeglasses

Black (and White) Ops

Renner's nearly dead cell phone provided just enough light to reveal the holder of the low card. Mason. Not the fittest of the squad, but perhaps the most motivated to accept the assignment.

The ghostly shadow of the huddled comrades flickered on the basement's cement wall and disappeared. Renner had managed to sneak the cell past the warden, but the charger was commandeered with his belongings. All that was left was one set of old walkies with batteries of an unknown age. Mason would take one on his mission while Watkins, the company's de facto communications officer, would be ready to assist as needed.

It had been over two hours since the blackout, and they had used that time wisely. Knowing they would have one chance and one chance only, each had presented his own concise, yet thorough, argument for the best use of their limited resources.

Ultimately, the vote was unanimous. Provisions were the top priority.

Prior to the room going dark, Theis had the layout memorized and was the rational choice to run logistics. He briefed Mason.

"Remember," Theis whispered. "There are switches everywhere once you get out of this room. Consider everything electronic as a potential silent alarm. Do you understand?"

Mason nodded. Directions memorized and the walkie firmly attached to his waistband, Mason began the exacting quest.

At the top of the stairs, Mason listened at the door. Nothing. He gingerly turned the knob, holding his breath against a tell-tale creak. The room appeared to be as pitch-black as the basement, but a flicker in the corner caught the guerilla's eye. Ambient light from a curtain opening was reflecting off a large metallic surface in the corner. It was a refrigerator. *Jackpot!*

He moved through the galley as if the wind, navigating by the sliver of light. At last, he saw the prize. As he reached for it, the ancient two-way radio slipped off and clattered across the floor. He heard noise from another area of the building and saw a light go on. Mason grabbed the booty, abandoned the device, and bolted, reversing the course to the basement.

The victorious warrior descended the stairs, clutching the spoils of his mission. He was greeted with high-fives and stage whispers of "mission accomplished!"

"What happened?" Watkins asked. "I've been calling you and no answer."

"The walkie fell and I had to abort," Mason said. "Luckily, I already had what I came for."

The group formed a circle and tore into the package of Double Stuffed Oreos just as the lights blazed on.

The warden stood at the top of the stairs, walkie in hand.

"Joshua Theis," she said. "It's one a.m. When you have a sleepover, lights out means lights out."

"I know. Sorry, Mom."

Mrs. Theis surveyed the group of terrorized, black-toothed eleven-year-olds and shook her head.

"Don't you boys know how to eat Oreos?" she asked. "Someone go upstairs and get the milk."

~ The Prompt ~

Category: Short Story
Genre: Thriller
Twist Sub-Genre: Techno-thriller
Event: Blackout

Switched at Death

Amber stared at the bag, hypnotized by each drop that fell into the tube leading to the port near her husband's shoulder. Not that long ago, "doxorubicin" would have seemed nothing more than a word for an expert crossword solver. But after nearly six months of bags with that label hung on the machine, she could write a paper on the powerful chemo drug.

When will this nightmare end? It was only half a year since Lowell's diagnosis, but holding vigil at his bedside, watching him decline ever faster as the treatment did nothing, made it feel like half a lifetime.

Until then, Lowell Masterson had everything money could buy. Besides properties, servants, and expensive toys, his money had bought the best divorce lawyer on the west coast. His first wife walked away after nearly forty years with little more than basic maintenance and the loyalty of their only child, Nicholas.

Lowell then shopped for a new, late-model wife, and Amber was in the right place at the right time. She came to California with stars in her eyes, but the beautiful twenty-eight-year-old was happy to settle for rings on her fingers and coke up her nose. So charmed was Lowell by the enchantress almost fifty years his junior that he made her his bride without even a thought of a prenup.

That was eight years ago, and while Amber enjoyed the many excesses the relationship provided, she had grown tired of the old man. But she knew if she tried to leave, she would have no better luck bringing any of Lowell's fortune with her than her predecessor had.

After they married, he had changed his trust to give everything to Amber. He hadn't excluded Nicholas outright, but a standard provision that Amber need only survive Lowell by thirty days seemed a guarantee that the son would get nothing. Amber decided to grit her veneers and stick it out. Then Christmas came early thanks to a November cat scan.

"Stage four liver cancer," the doctor stated with little emotion. Amber compensated with her own crocodile tears. *And they said I don't have what it takes to be an actress!*

"We can start chemotherapy," the doctor continued, "but be aware that it is aggressive and risky, especially to the heart. Nonetheless, we have seen many patients respond very well, so I think it's worth a try."

The estate was renovated to include a full hospital wing, with housing for staff, equipment, medicine, and supplies. Despite their prior estrangement, Nicholas visited his father once a week and enjoyed some of the father-son time that had been absent while Lowell was busy earning his fortune. Amber usually left them alone, grateful for a break from the tedium her marriage had become.

Today was an unscheduled visit for Nicholas. He had been summoned to his father's bedside, as the nurse on duty feared the end was near. Given the social status of his patient, the doctor was holding vigil as well.

"I really thought the chemo would buy him some time," Nicholas said, his words filled not with accusation, but sincere grief.

"Cancer is a strange beast," the doctor responded. "You just never know why chemo works for one person and not another."

Amber was dressed in her finest black suit, greeting guests who had come back to her home after the funeral. She saw Nicholas come in with a woman she couldn't quite place but was too busy playing the grieving widow to give it much thought.

Later that night, after the guests had gone, Nicholas found Amber sitting alone in the library. He came bearing a martini and a warm smile.

"You look like you could use this," he said.

"And how!" she replied, taking a big gulp. "Hey, who was that woman you came in with earlier. I think I know…"

Her eyes rolled back in her head, and Nicholas was able to grab both the glass and his wicked stepmother before either hit the floor.

Amber awoke in a bright, familiar room. She lay in a hospital bed, and as her vision cleared, she saw Nicholas and the woman at her bedside. It came to her. The woman was one of Lowell's nurses.

"What's going on?" Amber asked, confused and irritated. "Why am I here?"

"You fainted," Nicholas answered, with a telling grin. "I think it was something you drank."

Amber began to panic and tried to sit up but was caught on something. She turned to see an IV in her arm, with the tube snaking up to a clear bag on its usual hook. The label on the bag read "0.9% Sodium Chloride." The nurse walked over and flipped a switch.

Amber struggled to pull out the IV, but both of her arms were restrained. She screamed to no avail. The medical team and servants were long gone.

"What are you so upset about, Amber?" Nicholas said, strolling over to join the nurse at the machine. "It's just saline solution. We thought you might be dehydrated after all that crying and drinking today."

"No, please, turn it off!" Amber pleaded.

"You know what's funny about the IV bags in the storage area?" Nicholas continued, reaching for the bag. "Look how easily the labels come off."

He picked at the corner of the label with a fingernail, and it peeled away effortlessly.

"If someone wasn't paying close attention, a person could switch the labels between saline and any other bag… maybe even doxorubicin.

"Of course, someone with a trained eye," he added, turning to the nurse, "would spot the deception pretty fast."

"Please," she begged again. "I'll do anything. I'll split the money with you."

"It's not about the money," Nicholas answered. "My dad could see you didn't love him. You broke his heart.

"Now I'm going to break yours."

~ The Prompt ~

Category:
Short Story

Topic:
A container that holds something other than what its label says

Just Right

Bacon sizzled in the cast iron skillet, a savory snap, crackle, and pop that no cereal could match. Ellen removed the final slice and cracked an egg into the liquid gold in the pan.

As if following a cartoon ribbon of the mouthwatering aroma, Joseph walked in the back door.

"Feet!" Ellen said, without turning from the stove.

"Don't worry, I wiped them," Joseph said to his wife. He leaned into her back, squeezed her bottom, and whispered, "Morning, honey."

She smiled and turned to receive his good morning kiss; a ritual that had rarely been missed in their forty-five years of marriage.

Ellen spooned the fried eggs onto the plate of bacon and Joseph took it to the table. She'd already eaten, tackling the inside chores since dawn while Joseph milked cows, fed sheep, and shoveled out the barn.

She poured herself a cup of coffee and watched Joseph refuel his muscular six-foot, four-inch frame. Seven babies and years of pie making had left five-foot tall Ellen with a much different physique, but Joseph never seemed to notice.

"The kids are pretty excited about tonight," Joseph said. "They must have something big planned for our anniversary."

"I hope they don't go overboard," Ellen said. "There really isn't anything we need."

The dryer buzzed. "Back to work," she said, patting Joseph's hand.

"Me too." He took a last gulp of coffee.

"Allow plenty of time to clean up today, dear," Ellen instructed. "It's a fancy restaurant."

Ellen spread the warm patchwork quilt on their bed. The early 1800s farmhouse had three bedrooms. Once the children arrived, Ellen and Joseph took the smallest to allow for bunk beds in the others. Now empty nesters, they could have relocated but liked the coziness of the double bed—Joseph's overhanging feet notwithstanding.

***

"So," Joseph said, "this is how royalty lives."

He and Ellen's magnificent first day at Paradise Villa was almost over. At a perfectly executed surprise party, their kids had given them a weekend away in a luxury suite, complete with guest steward, private pool, hot tub, and room service, while promising to break out their overalls and take care of the farm.

Joseph helped Ellen out of the hot tub and into the plush hotel robe. "Living the high life is as tiring as chores. Let's go to bed."

An hour later, they were still wide awake on the California king mattress.

"I'm going to wake up and not be able to find you," Ellen said.

"It doesn't feel right," Joseph agreed.

The king mattress in the other bedroom was no better.

"I have an idea," Joseph said, gathering the silky duvet. "Follow me."

He led Ellen to the sitting room. The far end of the twelve-foot curved sofa featured a chaise lounge.

Joseph lay down first; on his side, ready to spoon. Ellen took her proper position. Joseph's feet hung off the end of the sofa and sleep came in minutes as they channeled their beloved patchwork quilt.

~ The Prompt ~

Category:
Flash Fiction

Genre:
There's Only One Bed

Location:
Luxury Villa

Character:
Farmer

The Day You Left Me

They always ask the same question on every anniversary. They've done it forever: Kennedy, the moon landing, Elvis. Hell, if they'd had cable news in 44 BC, a perky blonde in a toga would ask, "Where were you when Julius Caesar was stabbed?"

Me? I was checking out at Kings Food in Hoboken when the warning sirens went off. Everyone knew they tested the sirens the first *Wednesday* morning of the month. It wasn't a test.

It was the day you left me.

You were still in the shower that September 11. I was leaving early before the "no rainchecks" specials sold out. I remember yelling, "Love you! Have a good day!" through your bathroom door—but did I? Or is that a manufactured memory to ease grief and survivor's guilt? I don't know.

After the sirens, the store manager brought a portable TV from his office. We all crowded around the service desk to watch. That plane was sticking out of Tower One and I said, "Thank God Joe is in Tower Two." As they say, "From your lips to God's ears." Thanks for nothing, God.

It was impossible to get to you… and for what? Would I find you there? What good would it do to visit the gruesome site? I'd already been forced to watch losing you in real time.

So, I went home. No groceries. No husband. No hope.

I managed to function in the outside world, but was paralyzed inside our house. I wasn't curled up in the fetal position, but for months I couldn't bring myself to go through your things. It took me a week to put your last coffee cup in the dishwasher, and another three days to run it. I was finally able to face my new reality in the new year.

You know the rest. I opened your closet to find it empty. Just like your dresser, medicine cabinet, nightstand, and jewelry box. No, that's wrong; there were two things in the jewelry box: the expensive lighter I'd given you for your birthday and a sealed letter addressed to me. Dated 9/11, it said you were leaving, with a new woman and identity. "Don't bother trying to find me."

Believe me, I won't.

You see, once the dust settled, your employer—who is also providing health insurance to me in perpetuity, by the way—turned over your retirement funds to me. He was so sorry for my loss.

Then last year, I received two million dollars from the September 11th Victim Compensation Fund. What could I do? You can't fight City Hall.

And earlier this month you were finally declared legally dead. That's why I got another letter in today's mail. With a life insurance check for five million. Double indemnity, you know.

So yeah, I'm set. Of course, if someone found your letter, I'd lose everything and probably go to jail. Good thing you left the lighter.

Tonight, it's finally getting put to good use.

~ The Prompt ~

Category: Flash Fiction

Genre: Open

Action: Warning

Object: Sealed Envelope

Returning to the Scene of the Crime

A SWAT Team leader is forced to face his own demons when responding to an active shooter scenario at the high school he attended.

"Code Blue, all units. Active shooter reported at Berglund High School. I repeat. Code Blue, all units. Proceed to Berglund High School for active shooter response. This is not a drill."

"Ten-four," Lieutenant Benjamin Peck answered. "Ten-David ETA three minutes." He hit the lights and siren, made a U-turn, and tapped his earpiece to activate the dedicated channel to the members of his SWAT team.

"Assemble at assigned posts in full gear. Advise ETA."

The channel erupted in a cacophony of answers. Within five minutes, the full team had arrived, donned protective gear and weaponry, and ran to their pre-designated points of entry. Local squad cars from Berglund and surrounding towns formed a perimeter around the campus, waiting for instruction from SWAT.

As Ben prepared to give the order to enter the building, he caught a glimpse of the memorial in the lobby trophy case. It displayed photos of the teacher and four students killed in a 2005 school shooting and transported him back to his living room on that unforgettable day.

It was Ben's junior year, and the seventeen-year-old was not having the "successful high school career" expected of him by the administration. He was on the second day of a three-day out-of-school suspension. He had been caught again employing one of the many arrows in his quiver of cowardly bullying tactics.

The school sent him home, and his mother denied him access to all electronics and put him to work. The only mercy she showed (and for their mutual benefit) was keeping Ben's suspension from his father.

"We don't need to set him off any more than usual," she had told Ben, absentmindedly rubbing the fading bruise on her arm. "You just act like normal when he gets home from work and that'll be that."

Ben was putting towels away when his mother screamed for him to come downstairs. Like every afternoon, she had been sitting on the couch, chain smoking, and watching *All My Children.* The local television station had interrupted with a report of a shooter at the high school.

The TV showed an aerial shot of the school from the traffic helicopter. There was a large group of kids and teachers out on the lawn. Ben guessed they were from the exterior classrooms that had exit doors directly to the outside. Even at a distance, he could see people hugging, and one girl turned away from the group and vomited violently on the grass.

A reporter inside the helicopter narrated the scene.

"Something is happening near the main entrance. Someone—it looks like it could be a student—is running out of the front doors. He is carrying something—" The camera zoomed in. "It's some kind of large gun. Police are running after him. Other police outside are closing in. I don't think he expected any outside. He's lifting the gun—"

The crowd outside dropped to the ground and the station cut back to the reporter, a hand to her earpiece.

"Police report they have neutralized the suspected shooter, who can be seen lying on the sidewalk. Even from here, we can see a large pool of blood spreading beneath his head."

Ben turned to his mother, who shook her head before he even spoke.

"But Mom, I have to go there! I have to see if my friends are okay. I should be with them."

"I'm sure they're fine," his mother said. "You can talk to them when they get home. I'll let you use the phone, just for tonight. Now go back to your chores. It'll take your mind off of everything."

Ben knew arguing would do nothing, so he trudged up the stairs.

"And I don't want to hear any television on up there," his mother yelled. "Just concentrate on your work."

Three hours later, after Ben had been unable to reach anyone by phone, the doorbell rang. His friend Andy stood in the doorway; his eyes red. *Has he been crying? Nobody's cried since fifth grade.*

"Well, don't just stand there, come in," Ben said. "I've been calling everyone and—"

Andy rushed in and pulled Ben into a tight hug, sobbing into his shoulder.

"I'm so sorry, Ben. I'm so, so sorry."

Ben pulled away and looked at him.

"What are you talking about? Sorry about what?"

"Oh my God. You don't know, do you?"

Ben's earpiece crackled. "Everyone in place, sir." Before giving the command to deploy, he took one last look at the last picture in the memorial. Patrick Wentzel. His best friend. Killed by a school shooter twenty years ago.

The SWAT team moved like smoke down the quiet hallways, each man on high alert for the slightest noise or movement. Were it not for the helmets, face guards, shields, and automatic weapons, the group could be mistaken for a highly choreographed dance team.

Another crackle on the earpiece.

"Thirty-David reporting from southwest hallway. Victims are in classroom twenty-three. All appear dead. Blood smears in hall indicate shooter on the move toward the atrium."

"Ten-four," Ben said. "Implement formation to surround atrium. Hold your positions in the perimeter and hold your fire unless needed for defense. I will initiate negotiation tactics."

Ben peered into the atrium and saw the shooter taking cover behind a bench.

Jesus Christ, he can't be more than fourteen. The fucking gun looks like it weighs more than he does.

"This is Lieutenant Benjamin Peck. You are surrounded, but I have ordered all officers not to shoot. You are safe unless you take offensive action. Please set down your weapon and come out so we can talk."

"Bullshit!" the shooter yelled with a conspicuous lisp. "You're going to shoot the minute I come out."

"I am in charge and I told them all to stand down. Son, I give you my word."

"You're not my father," the shooter screamed.

"I know I'm not," Ben said. "But I care about what happens to you."

"You don't care; nobody cares."

"Believe me, I do. I've been through this before, and not as a policeman."

This apparently hit a nerve with the shooter. He stood up, still holding the gun.

"That's good," Ben said. "How about we meet in the middle here?"

"Okay, but I'm not putting down my gun."

"That's fine. Just keep it pointing at the floor and everything's good. You see, I'm doing the same, and so are my men."

Ben walked out of the hallway into the atrium. The shooter looked around and stepped carefully from the grassy area onto the tile.

"That's close enough," the shooter said.

"No problem. We can talk from here. What's your name, s—" He caught himself before saying "son."

"Jeremy."

"Okay, Jeremy. My goal is for all of us to leave this building alive, and with your help, we can reach that goal. That's it. Nobody else needs to die today. Understand?"

Jeremy looked at Ben for a long moment.

"What do you mean you've been through this before?"

It was Ben's turn for a thoughtful pause.

"Twenty years ago, I was a junior at this school. I was a bully and an asshole. It wasn't a good day unless I humiliated someone. If a girl wouldn't go out with me, or wouldn't put out when she did, I'd tape a picture of a dog to her locker. I'd pants freshmen boys and shove them into the girls' bathroom. And if you really crossed me, you could expect to open your locker on Monday to used tampons or shit—literal shit—on the inside."

Jeremy looked skeptical.

"Believe me," Ben said. "When you're the level of delinquent I was, I could break in anywhere, anytime. But it didn't stop there.

"Facebook had only been around for about a year, but I made the most of that too. I created a fake account so I wouldn't get caught. Now, instead of just a picture, I could go online and call those same girls ugly sluts. I made fun of kids with disabilities and posted gay and racial slurs. If I did a really good job, the victims would suspect someone else, and I'd get to watch the battle play out as my reward."

"And now you're a big shot cop," Jeremy said. "What, did you find Jesus or something?"

Jesus came out as "Jethuth."

"What happened was April 26, 2005. I'm guessing that's about five years before you were born."

Jeremy said nothing.

"That was the day that Enis Glover came to school with his father's semi-automatic hunting rifle hidden in his cello case. After band class, he went to the bathroom and waited for the next period to start. He then walked down to my fourth period chemistry class, opened the door, and started shooting.

"At first, no one knew what was happening. This was before school shooter drills were common. Anyway, he hit Mr. Jensen first, right in the face. The force pushed his mutilated head into the blackboard, and he slid down the wall, leaving a trail of bright red blood.

"Then he turned and sprayed the gun toward the lab tables. Some kids had dropped to the floor or tried to get out of their seats to run. In the end, he killed four students. One of them was my best friend, Patrick. He was sitting next to his girlfriend and was pushing her to the floor when he took multiple shots to the back. He saved her life."

"Were you hit?" Jeremy asked.

Ben looked down at the floor and then back up at Jeremy.

"I wasn't there."

Ben swallowed hard and continued.

"You see, even though I thought I was a master criminal and untouchable, I had been caught in the act for a second time and was home on a three-day suspension. I got the details later from a friend who was also in the class.

"Want to know the irony of it, Jeremy? Guess who I was bullying when they caught me?"

"The shooter?"

"Yep, Enis Glover. Of course, I never called him by his real name. I alternated between Enis the Penis, just plain Penis, or my favorite, Penis Lover. I was writing that on his gym locker when I was caught."

"What happened to him?"

"He was shot and killed trying to escape. So you see, Jeremy, not only did I lose my best friend, I caused three—actually *four*—other kids and a great teacher to be killed too. Not to mention the pain I caused his family, the school, and the community."

"You don't know it was your fault."

In a normal negotiation, Ben would have recognized these questions as a successful chink in the shooter's armor; an opportunity to disarm him. But this retelling of his personal horror had caused his own armor to weaken.

"After everything happened, his mother found his journal. He said he was tired of being picked on, and he was going to show his dad and everyone else that people like him—who were in band or chess club, who liked different things than the jocks and popular kids…" He looked Jeremy right in the eye. "…or who had speech impediments—that they could be every bit as tough as them.

"Yeah, he didn't mention me by name, but it was my fault."

"So, you became a cop to make up for what you caused?" Jeremy asked.

"No," Ben said. "Nothing could ever make up for that, and I'll never forgive myself for being a bully, for pushing Enis until he snapped, and for not being there to save my friends. Never.

"But I figured I had to do my part to keep it from ever happening again. I don't want any more unnecessary deaths. And that includes yours."

Ben knew that every member of SWAT was an expert marksman, and though he had ordered them to hold their fire, he knew they wouldn't hesitate to disobey that order if Jeremy made a move that looked threatening. The next interaction was critical.

"What do you think, Jeremy? How about we all walk out of here alive?"

"I'm dead anyway, once I'm found guilty."

"Maybe," Ben said. "But there's more than your life at stake depending on what you do right now."

"What do you mean?"

"Take a good look at the other cops around the room," Ben said.

Jeremy saw seven men in full combat gear, their fingers on the trigger of weapons that could be raised and fired in an instant.

"All eight of us have shot to kill more than once," Ben continued. "We knew we'd have to when we signed up, and we do it without hesitation when the situation calls for it.

"But here's the thing, Jeremy. Every time we kill someone, it kills a little bit inside of us too. I'm asking you to end the killing right here and now. What do you say?"

Jeremy began to sob. He set the gun down on the floor and was instantly swarmed by the other team members.

"Take it easy on him, guys," Ben said. "He's going peacefully."

Ben radioed they would be bringing the suspect out alive through the main entrance. Jeremy's wrists and ankles were shackled, and he was pulled to his feet.

"Standard formation, men. I will escort the suspect," Ben said.

A dozen uniforms were waiting in the main lobby when the SWAT team arrived. As Ben released the shooter to their custody, he noticed Jeremy staring at the memorial display before turning back to Ben and mouthing, "I'm sorry."

The lobby was instantly flooded with medical and police personnel from all departments. The SWAT member who passed the crime scene led a group to the classroom. The Chief of Police and Coroner were in an animated conversation with the heads of the Crisis Management and Public Information departments, while homicide detectives and crime scene investigators were jockeying for position.

Amid the chaos, Ben stood and stared at the memorial display, wiping tears from his eyes.

I can't ever make it up to you, Patrick. But I hope this is a start.

~ The Prompt ~

Category: Short Story

Genre: Action/Adventure

Theme: Teamwork

Character: Reformed Bully

A Second Career for the Ages

They say no one wants to work anymore.
But everyone's dying to get a job at PRU.

The bus chugged up the steep incline of the hill, slowly approaching incandescence so brilliant even astronomers might think it a misplaced Aurora Borealis. At the crest, the source of the light was equally ethereal—an industrial complex that ostensibly stretched into space itself, its blazing streetlights becoming pinpoints mingling with the stars.

The driver switched on his microphone. "We'll be there soon. Stay together when you get off and wait for instructions."

The customary rustling such announcements usually provoked was not forthcoming. Instead, the fifty or so men and women sat silently, staring straight ahead like one giant, slightly confused, deer in the headlights.

The group huddled outside the main entrance. Matching battleship gray uniforms conjured an image of a beached whale longing to get back to the sea. They were herded into the building by an authoritative-looking woman. Her badge simply said "Marjorie" under the PRU logo.

"Good morning," she announced, "and welcome to the start of your new life's work. Of course, we won't know what that is until our experts have assessed your experience, interests, and abilities. That's where our one-of-a-kind, in-house training facility does its magic."

She turned her gaze to the right, and the assemblage followed suit.

Brows furrowed; they saw the foot-high letters over the doorway: **Screening – Placement – Training**.

Two PRU workers watched with amusement. "Nobody ever sees it coming," one said. "You'd think some word would have gotten to them by now."

"They wouldn't believe it anyway," the other replied. "I wonder if they'd try to fight it if they did." They shrugged and walked away.

Marjorie continued her speech.

"When your name is called, you will meet with Peter Nacre, our screening specialist. He's an expert at making sure everyone ends up in just the right place, and he will assign both your new job and the related training. Any questions?"

A young man raised his hand.

"I thought we were getting jobs, not training," he said. "What's the deal?"

"There's plenty of work and you'll be doing it soon," Marjorie explained. "But the work is so important—life changing, really—we can't take a chance with on-the-job training. So, we've created a school within our facility—near-the-job training, if you will—to ensure your competence before you get your first assignment. Peter will explain further when you meet him.

"Any other questions?" she asked and did not wait for an answer. "Good! Please sit down and wait to be called."

Peter Nacre scrolled through the list on the screen. This was an unusually good batch. He chuckled. *You can always count on that full moon.*

He pressed the intercom button. "Nancy, please send in Darin Marshall."

Minutes later a tall, tattooed man of about fifty came into the office. Peter asked him to sit down and went back to his computer screen. "So, Darin, I see that you've been a mechanic for many years," Peter said.

"Since I was sixteen," Darin said with pride, somehow further pumping up his already bursting abs. "I've never wanted to do anything else. I'm not quite sure why I'm looking for a new job."

"We'll get to that in due time, Darin. But tell me, since you're a mechanic, I assume you work in a noisy environment and spend a great deal of time manipulating heavy, unsteady metal objects. Is that right?"

"Sure, but what does that have to do with—"

"Very good," Peter said. "I think we have just the spot for you." He jotted a letter and number on a card, stood, and handed it to Darin.

"Go through that door and give this card to the woman at the desk and she'll get you to the right spot. A pleasure having you with us."

Darin's puzzled expression remained, but he stood and followed directions. Peter returned to his computer screen.

"Nancy, please send in Lois Custer."

An attractive woman of about sixty entered Peter's office with an elegance and flair that even industrial coveralls couldn't diminish. She extended a manicured hand to Peter before taking a seat.

"Tell me, Lois, what do you like best about interior design?"

"Everything!" she answered. "When I was a little girl, the first thing I did with my Barbie dreamhouse was rearrange the furniture! I haven't stopped since. The look on people's faces when they come into a room I've done… it's just priceless." She paused. "That's why I'm really confused."

"About what?" Peter asked.

"Well, why in the name of Nate Berkus would I ride on a *bus* to apply for a job at a *factory*?" Peter thought she might have thrown up a little in her mouth on that last word.

"Oh, Lois, we are so much more than a *factory*," he said, trying to match her disdain in his own inflection. "Believe me, if your career goal is to rearrange furnishings for the rest of time, you have come to the right place!"

Before she could ask or protest any further, Lois was handed her own card and sent to the next station. Peter summoned Joe Fredricks.

A tall, white-haired man took his time ambling into the office.

Peter knew at once that it was attitude, not age, that informed his gait and couldn't quite muster the informality to use his first name. "Mr. Fredricks, it's a pleasure to meet you. Please tell me a little about yourself and your interests."

"First and foremost, I'm an apiculturist," Joe replied, watching Peter closely. No recognition. "You don't do crossword puzzles, do you, young man?" he continued, his smile growing wider.

"No, sir, I don't."

"Then let me put in layman's terms," Joe said. "I'm a beekeeper."

Peter returned the smile. "I've always heard that was a fascinating hobby. What attracted you to it?"

"Well, young man, I worked for forty-five years at the post office. Inside, no windows, just noise and paper and dumbass government rules and red tape. Every night I'd go home and my wife would have to force me to come inside for bed.

"One of those nights I'm sitting on the back porch after dinner, and I see a bee—one single bee—inside a flower. It didn't pay me no mind, let me sit and watch. It was somethin' to see. Me and my wife talk about it and she says why don't you see what you need to be a beekeeper.

"Well, I think she's crazy. I tell her, you gotta be out in the country on a farm or something with lots of space away from people to have bees. So, goddammit the next day if she doesn't go straight to the library and get a book on beekeeping and prove me wrong. First time for everything, I always say."

They both laugh.

"You sure you want to hear about all this, young man?" Joe asks.

"It's the best story I've heard all day," Peter replies. "Don't stop now."

"Okay then. Well, a few years later it's time for me to retire from that hellhole, and I tell her, I don't want a party, no party. So, what does she do. She gives me a party. Our kids and grandkids are ALL there, and other people, and when it comes time to open presents—I told her I don't want no presents, mind you, but she listened to that about as well as she listened to anything else—so, when it's time to open presents, we all walk out into our tiny back yard and what do you think is sitting there?"

"A beekeeping, uh, *thing*," Peter guesses.

"Close enough," Joe says after a belly laugh. "Yeah, a beekeeping *thing*, and all the stuff to get me started. The wife even got into it after a while. Took us almost 50 years of marriage, but we finally found a hobby we both liked." He stopped abruptly and stared into space.

"Mr. Fredricks?" Peter said gently.

"Those damn bees are all that's kept me going since my wife died last year. Those goddamn bees."

Peter gave Joe a moment.

"So, tell me, Mr. Fredricks, what do you think you'd like to do now?"

"About what?"

"Your next job," Peter replied. "What do you think would interest you?"

"Job? I already told you; I'm retired. I don't want another job. Is that why they made me get on that goddamn bus? To get another job?"

"Mr. Fredricks, if I may ask, how old are you?"

"I'll be 92 next month," Joe answered. "Don't you think that's too damn old for a job?"

"I certainly do, Mr. Fredricks," Peter apologized. "There's clearly been some mistake."

"I thought I got on a bus to meet my daughter to look at some stupid retirement home. I told her I don't want to go to no retirement home, but she listens just like her mother listened, which means she don't. I'm not going nowhere that I can't have my bees." He looked Peter right in the eye.

"And I don't want no job either, young man!"

"Don't worry about that another moment, Mr. Fredricks," Peter assured. "But I may be able to help you find a new place to live where you could keep your bees."

Joe perked up.

"Our organization has many branches, and one offers a marvelous relocation service. In fact, I have it on good authority that you could move into a new home in the middle of one of the most beautiful gardens anyone has ever seen. It will be a perfect place for you and your bees."

After Joe was on his way, Peter quickly assessed and dispatched several more candidates: an HVAC contractor, a cardiologist, a YouTube cooking phenom, and even a snake handler. Never two days the same in Peter's office.

Jennifer Simmons was Peter's last interview of the day. The thirty-something brunette exhibited an inner strength that contradicted her perky demeanor and small stature.

"How has your day been?" she asked as she took her seat.

"Very good, thanks, and yours?" Peter replied.

"Oh, it's pretty exciting when you have three kids under six," Jennifer said. "They sure keep me on my toes."

Peter's stomach began to clench. *Every time I think I've made it through the day, this happens.*

"I'm sure your husband is a big help," Peter offered.

"Well, between you and me, he's pretty helpless," Jennifer confided, with an embarrassed smile. "Don't get me wrong, he has a great job and he's very smart, but when it comes to the house and the kids, I don't know if he'd make it a day without me. But don't tell him I said that. I'd never want to hurt his feelings. So, why am I here? I don't think I have time for a job."

"Actually, Jennifer, you do. And it's a very special one. Almost no one who comes through this office qualifies. Let's take a walk and I'll help get you started."

Peter led Jennifer out into the giant, open classroom. Those who had passed through his office earlier were already deep into their training, having traded their gray uniforms for the flowing black robes they would wear for eternity.

Darin is rattling chains under the careful tutelage of an experienced ghost.

"That's good, but a little more clanking, and hold that oooooh just a little longer and try to time it between the big clanks. Don't worry, you'll get it."

Mansion-style curtains are being surreptitiously blown around by the HVAC guy. "All that time I wasted installing duct work!" he says to his teacher.

"Can I pick who I haunt?" Lois asks excitedly, as she uses her newfound powers to rearrange knickknacks on a shelf across the room. "I know just who deserves it first!"

Peter and Jennifer pass similar classes, finally arriving at a white door. They enter, and a lovely woman is waiting with white robes for Jennifer.

"This is for you, my dear," she says. "It's a privilege not many are afforded."

Jennifer looks from the woman to Peter, finally realizing what's happened.

"I'm dead," she says. "I'm never going to see my family again, and now I have to be a ghost and haunt people." She begins to cry.

"Yes, you are a ghost," the woman says, helping Jennifer into the white robes. "But the rest isn't true. You will see your family, although they won't see you. However, they will feel your presence every minute. You are not being sent to haunt, but to heal."

Peter bids Jennifer farewell and heads toward the main auditorium, stopping on his way to peek into the Garden of Eden, where Joe and his wife are tending his beloved bees.

It's graduation day, and he arrives just in time to see a large group of ghosts, clad in the familiar black robes, being released to begin their assignments.

"Congratulations, Graduates" is announced, and they fall into formation to levitate and then fly to and through the wall of the auditorium.

Outside, the formation banks to the left and individual ghosts begin to break off and go toward their assignments. As the last ghost makes a final turn, the side of the facility comes into view, an otherworldly mist tickling the bottom of the neon sign proclaiming the company name: Poltergeists R Us.

~ The Prompt ~

Category:
Short story

Genre:
Ghost Story

Subject:
Vestibule School

Character:
Beekeeper

Two for the Road

They say you can find anything at the World's Largest Truck Stop. Sometimes even love.

Emily descended to the main floor of Iowa 80, her hair still glistening from the luxurious hot shower. She had pushed right through to the very end of her sixteen-hour limit the night before, pulling the tractor trailer into the truck stop just ahead of the predicted blizzard. After straggling in for a bathroom break and snack, she crashed in her truck and awoke eight hours later to the expected blanket of snow, unsafe driving conditions, and a rare opportunity to loiter before getting back on the road.

She surveyed the panorama that was the World's Largest Truck Stop, off I-80 near the otherwise insignificant hamlet of Walcott, Iowa. *Luck 'o the Irish comes through again. I'm at Mall of America instead of camping out behind some filthy gas station.*

That mental image reminded her she needed a birthday gift for her niece. With countless shopping options spread out in all directions, Emily guessed the quadrant bordered by t-shirts, stuffed animals, and toys would be the best place to start.

"Shopping for yourself or a friend?" Emily, startled, turned around.

"Oh, sorry. I didn't mean to scare you," the young woman said. "I noticed you've been kind of going back and forth in this area for a while and thought maybe you could use some help."

Emily relaxed and smiled.

"Could I ever," she replied. "Why is it so hard to find something for a twelve-year-old girl? For God's sake, I used to be one!"

"Well, I'm not sure the twelve-year-olds today are anything like the twelve-year-olds we were. That could be part of it.

"I'm Sara, by the way," she continued, extending a hand. "You stranded, too?"

"Yeah, for a while," Emily said. "I think that's my problem. Usually I run in, pee, buy what I need, and am back on the road right away. The snow is giving me too much time to think."

Sara glanced at a shelf behind Emily and gestured. "Take a look at that."

They walked over to the "Mystery Cube" display, where piles of nondescript, black boxes filled the shelves. Sara grabbed a pamphlet and read:

Do you have secrets to keep? Things to hide? Nosy brothers who keep reading your diary? Then you need a Mystery Cube.

"Sounds like just what a twelve-year-old girl needs," Emily said. "How does it work?"

Even if your enemy realizes that this plain old cube holds your precious secrets, they will never get inside. There is a screen on the bottom of the cube that needs a password…

Emily picked up one of the cubes and turned it over. Both noticed a small screen, just as described, flashing "enter password."

The password is continually changing. When you download the Mystery Cube app and register your cube, you and only you will have access to the password.

“Sold!” Emily said. “Nosy brothers be damned!”

Both laughed and headed to the register together.

“Have you had breakfast yet?” Emily asked. “My treat. Without your eagle eye I’d still be shopping long after the plows had gone through.”

“That sounds great,” Sara said. “I don’t know the last time I had a meal that wasn’t in a to-go bag.”

The Iowa 80 Kitchen—the truck stop’s only sit-down restaurant—was packed with stranded motorists, but Emily and Sara found a cozier-than-usual table for two and ordered.

Over coffee and a delicious midwestern feast, the two women compared stories… of their interests, career choice, life on the road, dreams, and families.

“My mother was horrified that I was going to be a trucker,” Emily said. “She told me, ‘I can’t even call you a lady trucker because there is nothing ladylike about it.’ She grudgingly came around when she realized maybe this would mean I’d *finally* meet a man and settle down. Pretty funny, huh?"

Their eyes met and they shared a knowing gaze for a few seconds. Sara looked down at the table.

“You know, some of us could have really used that Mystery Cube back in the day. In fact, when it comes to my family, I could still use it now.”

She looked back up at Emily, whose face was the picture of sympathy and understanding. She placed her hand lightly on Sara’s.

“Not everyone needs to know our secrets, Sara,” she said. “As long as we are true to ourselves, that’s all that matters.”

Sara blinked moist eyes and looked over Emily’s shoulder. The restaurant was nearly empty.

“Looks like we outlasted the storm,” Sara said. “I hate to say it, but we probably should get back on the road.”

“Yep,” Emily said, standing up. “Where you headed?”

“I’m going west to Omaha,” Sara answered as they walked out of the restaurant. “I go back and forth between there and Chicago a couple times a week. You?”

"East to Toledo, then back to Des Moines," Emily replied. "I make that haul a couple times a week too."

They stopped and turned to face each other, both smiling broadly.

"There's a lot of overlap between Des Moines and Chicago," Emily said, moving just a little closer to Sara.

"Don't you think I know that?" Sara replied with mock sarcasm. "After all, I am a 'lady trucker.'"

They visited the ladies' room and headed out to their rigs. Amazingly, despite the nine hundred parking spots for trucks, they were in the same row, with just a handful of vehicles in between.

Sara walked Emily to her truck.

"Thank you," she said. "And not just for breakfast."

Before Emily could respond, Sara leaned forward and kissed her with unabashed confidence. She pressed something into Emily's hand and ran to her truck.

Emily looked at the paper and climbed into the semi. Within a few minutes, she was back on I-80 and grabbed the CB microphone.

"Breaker, breaker," she said. "This is Lady Trucker looking for Mystery Cube. Do you copy?"

~ The Prompt ~

Category: Short Story

Genre: Rom Com - Meet Cute

Object: Mysterious Box

Character: Trucker

Tenure of the Heart

Paula collapsed onto the wooden bench. Wrangling her rolling suitcase and shoulder bag down the steps from her third-floor walk-up, then on and off the CTA bus, had exhausted her before she even got to Union Station. She looked at her wrist.

Dammit. What else did I forget?

She glanced around the terminal and found the huge wall clock, looking like a Medieval rondel high on the ornately carved station wall. Ten after seven.

About twenty minutes to boarding. I should let Mom know I made the early train.

She texted her ETA and did some people watching. Weary travelers lugging suitcases plodded by while commuters—carrying only expensive coffee and corporate stress—moved at a quicker pace, somehow dodging the masses while hypnotized by their iPhone screens.

Paula felt like she was in a time-lapse movie sequence where the main character is standing still, unnoticed, while people speed by in a blur. But it wasn't the train station causing the sensation. It was her mother's call yesterday afternoon.

"What's wrong, Mom?" Her mother knew cell phone use during class was unprofessional and she wouldn't call unless it was an emergency.

"Dad had a heart attack, and it's serious," her mom had said, never one to ease into bad news. "You need to get here right away."

Paula went straight to the principal and was on the 'L' fifteen minutes later.

Say what you want about Chicago Public Schools, but they take care of their own.

She couldn't make the last train to Urbana yesterday and cursed her friends' bad advice—and herself—for taking it.

"You won't need a car if you live and work in the city." Ugh! I'd be there already if I had a car. Mom needed me last night, and I need to see Dad.

The PA system crackled.

"Now boarding on Track 11, Amtrak Saluki Train 391 to Champaign-Urbana. All ticketholders please report to Track 11 for immediate boarding."

Paula slung her backpack and purse over her shoulder and made her way to the track, pulling the rolling suitcase behind her. She walked through the coach car, grateful she had splurged on a business class seat for the two-and-a-half-hour ride. A baby was crying and she knew it wouldn't be long before you could cut the tension with a knife in the cheap seats.

She settled in and opened her backpack, grabbing a protein bar and the stack of writing assignments she needed to grade. She took a bite and picked up Miranda's. The twelve-year-old was one of the standout writers in her seventh-grade class.

> The 1968 Illinois Earthquake Was a Big One!
> If you think earthquakes only happen in California your wrong! One of the biggest recorded earthquakes in all of the midwest United States happened at 11:02 am in the morning on November 9 in 1968 and it was a 5.4 on the Rickter scale and it was so big that the shaking was felt in 23 states of more than a half a million miles of land. It caused scientists to find a new fault line in southern Illinois and scientists say that theres a 90 percent chance that there

could be another huge earthquake like 6-7 on the Rickter scale before 2055 in Illinois.

Paula took out a red pen, added some punctuation, circled misspelled words, and wrote "beware of run-on sentences!" in the margin.

If Miranda's paper was this rough, the rest are going to be brutal. But dad will get a kick out of reading these young Hemingways.

She pulled out the next paper and quickly returned it to the bag. Her heart wasn't in it; all she could think about was Dad.

He would never admit it, but I know he wanted a boy. Why else would they name me Paula? I may be an English teacher, but I can still put two and two together.

She smiled. Neither she nor Mom ever had any interest in Girl Scouts, and, in those days, only boys were in Boy Scouts. So, Dad found Indian Princesses, a father-daughter organization that did the same kind of things that the Scouts did, except Mom was off the hook.

I wonder if they're still allowed to use that name these days. Whatever; if Dad couldn't have a son, he was determined to do all those father and son things with a daughter. And we had a ball. Oh my God, that time we went camping in early April and it snowed! There we were in K-Mart—that's a blast from the past—with all the dads buying us bathing suits so we could swim at the motel. Dad loved to tell everybody about our adventure at Camp Ramada Inn. Holy cow. I think Dad invented glamping!

What Paula loved most in Indian Princesses were the baseball games. And not just playing; more than that she loved watching her father—every inch the stereotypical, non-athletic, patches-on-his-elbows English professor he was—forcing himself out of his comfort zone to coach the team.

If Dad ever played or even watched baseball in his life, I'm the Queen of England. But he knew I loved it, so he tried to love it too.

The same was true ten years later when Paula brought Brian home. Although they were the picture of discretion and good manners, her parents didn't like him and she knew it. She had followed in Dad's footsteps and majored in education, but instead of attending U of I, where her father taught, she enrolled in Southern Illinois University, just over three hours away. Granted, it was renowned in the education arena, but Paula's main reason was to experiment with the tiniest bit of rebellion.

When she told them she was bringing home a boyfriend from college, Paula's parents assumed it was a teacher, or other professional-to-be, and were thrilled. Brian was, in fact, a nothing-to-be, and proud of it. A local who had barely scraped through high school, he hung around campus hoping to resurrect the university's party school reputation. After years in the stoic, intellectual atmosphere of her childhood home, Paula was attracted to this bad boy like a moth to the flame.

As often happens, her parents' objections only strengthened her resolve to stand by her man. Their wedding was a month after graduation, and although her parents never stopped trying to change her mind ("We can turn around right now," Dad had said at the back of the church), they also were gracious and gave no indication to the hundred guests that they weren't celebrating just as much on the inside as they were on the outside.

Three years later Paula and Brian divorced. She had been terrified to face her parents with the news they had known all along to be inevitable. She worried for nothing.

Never once did either of them say "I told you so." *They just took me in and let me wallow until we all could pretend it never happened. What a great summer that had been.*

While her mother, an accountant (one of those pesky, all-year jobs) was at work, Paula and her father reveled in their literary geekdom. Every afternoon they made their way to the "Al Fresco Reading Room" (their fancy name for the gazebo in the middle of the garden) and talked books.

Some kids had a secret club that met in a tree fort. I was the president and chief operating officer of the Walter and Paula Winninger Anybody is Welcome but Not Really Outdoor Summer Book Club. Then in the winter, or when it rained, there was the Walter and Paula Winninger Off-season Indoor Book Club and we didn't even pretend that anyone else was welcome to that.

The train car went over a rough crossing, and Paula grabbed her bag before the contents spilled on the floor. She grunted slightly as she repositioned it on the seat.

You know, I have a bad shoulder thanks to you, Dad. I can't go anywhere without at least three books, just in case I have a minute to read. Everyone tells me I'm nuts because I can bring my Kindle or read them on my phone. But you taught me that nothing beats a real book, and that's the kind of brainwashing that's here to stay. Thank God.

One of the strict rules growing up was a non-negotiable bedtime along with Dad's nightly mantra: "And no reading under the covers."

I was almost to the point of not having a bedtime before I realized Dad's strategy. Funny how there were always D batteries when I needed them for my flashlight.

The connecting door opened, and a bedraggled-looking woman stepped through. She was carrying a baby that looked to be about a year old, with two other preschool kids following exhibiting varying degrees of obedience. It was their own little marching band of chaos; thankfully, they exited through the opposite door as fast as they had appeared.

Paula thought about the day she found out why she was an only child.

What was I, maybe eighth grade? I had just come from Jenny Porter's house. She had two sisters and a brother. Their house was a mess and so much fun. Her mom was cool and laid back and they always had junk food. I came home and felt like I'd really been gypped because I didn't have any brothers or sisters. Our house was so quiet and no fun and neither Mom nor Dad was cool… Jeez, the martyrdom I spewed! So, being a teenage girl, I decided to take it out on Mom.

At first, she just tried to say, "no reason; it just happened that way." But I was a snotty bitch and kept pushing and saying things like, "was there something wrong with one of you?" and "normal families have more than one kid" and "I know Dad wanted a boy," and, finally, "how selfish could you be?"

She just sat down and put her head in her hands and started crying. I'd never seen her cry. I knew I'd gone too far, but it was too late. I said, "I'm sorry, Mom. Never mind." But she just kept crying, and after a couple of minutes, Dad came in from his study to see what all the yelling and crying was about.

Paula shuddered and wiped away a tear of her own.

I never saw Dad so mad, before or after. When he found out what happened, he just screamed at me. Screamed!

"Your mother almost died giving birth to you. Yes, we wanted more children, and it was heartbreaking for both of us. Sometimes it still is. But your mother's life was more important than you having a brother or sister. Don't you think so too?"

By then, I was also sobbing. "Of course, I do," I'd blubbered. "I'm sorry."

"You should be sorry. And what's been so bad about your life? You seem to have things pretty good around here. If you want to know about being selfish, go to your room and look in the mirror."

I thought he hated me and I knew he'd never speak to me again. But they both forgave me, and after a while, it was kind of forgotten. I know I was just a dumb, selfish kid, but they were more understanding than they needed to be. Well, now's my chance to finally make it up to them. Mom said Dad was going to need open-heart bypass surgery. I know that's a big deal.

She took out her phone and Googled "open-heart bypass." What she found was terrifying. The surgery itself was major but had become routine. Her dad was at the university's teaching hospital, so he was in good hands. But the care at home, along with the possible complications, was overwhelming.

Mom can't do this alone, even with visiting nurses. Time to step up.

Paula's über-organized teacher gene kicked into high gear. She opened her notebook to a fresh page and started the list:

1. Contact HR about taking FMLA.

2. Get copy of Mom and Dad's insurance to review in-home services.

3. Order cardiac diet cookbook.

4.

Her phone rang.

"Hi Mom, I think I'm about halfway—"

"Dad's gone."

Paula dropped her notebook and slumped in the seat.

"Oh, Mom. No. What happened?"

"We were sitting there, just talking, and he started having massive chest pain. Then the machine started screeching just like on TV. It was cardiac arrest. They all ran in and worked on him for over an hour, but he never woke up again."

Both women were crying now.

"Do you know the last thing he said before he collapsed?"

"What?"

"I can't wait to see Paula."

The words caught in her mother's throat and in Paula's heart.

"Is anyone with you, Mom? I should be there in about an hour."

"The chaplain is here. I'm okay. Be careful and I'll see you whenever you get here. I love you, honey."

"Love you too, Mom. I'll be there soon."

Paula cried for a few minutes then composed herself. She picked up her notebook from the floor, tore off and crumpled the earlier list, and started a new one.

1. Call provost.

2. See if Dad had prepaid burial.

3. What kind of service?

4. Eulogy.

She stopped. The eulogy. That couldn't be left to just anyone.

We didn't have any official by-laws, but I'm sure that one of the duties of the president and chief operating officer of the Walter and Paula Winninger Anybody is Welcome but Not Really Outdoor Summer Book Club is to write and deliver the eulogy for any other of the Club's distinguished members. First, it needs a title.

Paula turned the page in her notebook to a clean sheet, thought for a moment, and wrote across the top of the page:

"Books, Baseball, and the Professor Who Went to Bat for Me."

~ The Prompt ~

Category: Short Story

Character: teacher

Setting: train or train station

Must include: an earthquake

Ordering off the Menu

Unrequited love always leaves a bad taste in the mouth.

My darling, my beloved, how your absence makes me ache.
All day I dream about you while at night I lay awake
And dwell upon that fateful day you came into my life.
How unequivocal it was you'd someday be my wife.

"Hello, my name is Sarah, I'll be serving you today."
Your captivating beauty simply carried me away.
You positively sparkled as you took my order down;
Your waitress costume magically became a wedding gown.

I soon became a "regular" upon the diner stool
But it was not the chicken parm that caused my mouth to drool.
I wondered if you felt the same; if I should ask you out.
And then one day you touched my arm—there wasn't any doubt.

I figured I would start out slow, give things a chance to brew
Some small romantic gestures and you'd soon say "I love you."

A surreptitious twenty helped me gain your home address
I glimpsed you through your window—positively luminesce!
That's where I sent you love notes, pledging passion through
    and through,
But being coy I dutifully signed them "you know who."

And yet my efforts seemed in vain when I walked
    through the door
Your greeting was no different than it was the day before.
In fact, your mood had changed. You were no longer filled
    with glee.
Your happiness depended now entirely on me.

At last, I had the answer; it would fit just like a glove.
A monumental gesture to befit my boundless love.
I knew exactly what to do, it would be fast and clean
And you would feel my boundless love when
    witnessing the scene.

And so, on Meatloaf Monday, just like any other day
I parked my car and walked right in but had something to say.
No, not with words, there was no need; I stood and
    looked around
The RK-47 made a rat-a-tat-tat sound.

When it was done just you and I were left within the place.
I was surprised to see the awful look upon your face.
I won't say I regret a thing; I've thought it through and through.
I'd do it ten times over; I'd do anything for you.

This ends my weekly letter. I will write again real soon.
And please write back, that would be for my spirits quite a boon.
I'm sure by now you know the way to get the mail to me.
Send it to Inmate 14796813.

~ The Prompt ~

Category: Rhyming Short Story
Genre: Romance
Theme: Postal
Emotion: Unapologetic

Once Upon a Time
in a Church Basement Far, Far Away

"We have time for one more share," says Mother Goose. "What about you, dear?"

The newcomer nods.

"My name is Snow and I'm an Angerholic."

"Hi, Snow!" the dozen princesses chant.

"My mother died when I was born, and Father married a horrible woman."

"Same old, same old," Cinderella whispers to Ariel.

"I ran away and moved in with these seven pint-sized weird guys. One's a grouch, two never stop smiling, one's afraid of me, and the 'doctor' can't cure the sneezer or the narcoleptic. If you put it in a story, nobody would believe it.

"They work in a coal mine and come home every night like a hoard of wild animals, filthy and hungry. Last night, they're puffing away on their pipes and there's a knock at the door. It's some 'prince' who's telling me it's my lucky day because he's rescuing me.

"Between that and the Inelegant Seven, I snapped. Next thing you know the cops were there and hi ho, hi ho, it's off to anger management I go."

"You've come to the right place," says Sleeping Beauty. "Now, I think it's time we let you in our little secret."

Snow looked around the room; each princess wore a satisfied and knowing smile.

"Angerholics Anonymous is a front," Sleeping Beauty continues. "We're the PLL—Princess Liberation League."

"I washed that man right outta my hair years ago," says Rapunzel.

"We've developed our own specialized Twelve-Step Program," Belle says. "Be our guest?"

"Of course!" Snow says. "What's Step One?"

"We're taking you to our favorite movie," says Jasmine. "You can hitch a ride on my carpet."

"What movie?"

Mother Goose smiles. "*Barbie*, of course."

~ The Prompt ~

Category:
Micro Fiction

Genre:
Fairy Tale and/or Fantasy

Action:
Having a Tantrum

Word:
Hoard

"…and the horse you rode in on."

Secrets and unpleasant surprises are often the cause of a divorce. But when they're part of the divorce proceedings, anything can happen.

"Oh my God! What happened to you?"

"Don't ask," Robyn Porter said. She passed the mahogany reception desk and headed for the kitchen. Minutes later she was at her desk, holding a makeshift icebag on her bulging lower lip. She ran her free hand through her hair, felt something weird, and pulled it out. A piece of straw.

Just what all the best and brightest young lawyers in Chicago are accessorizing with this season. So much for this being my career-building lucky day.

It was one of the firm's highest-profile divorce cases and Robyn was thrilled the partners had entrusted it to her. John and Mary Ann Bergen, a North Shore power couple worth nearly ten million dollars, had been married sixteen years when everything suddenly fell apart.

Because their prenup had expired, John and Mary Ann hired attorneys to negotiate splitting the estate. Both played nice until one piece of personal property created an immovable stumbling block—a saddle.

Robyn adjusted the ice pack on her lip and shook her head.

A saddle. Not some saddle-shaped solid gold artifact from the Mesopotamian era. Not the actual apparatus worn by Secretariat in the Triple

Crown. No. An old, stinking, dirty, run-of-the-mill saddle. Well, if they want to spend $600 an hour fighting over a $500 saddle, that's up to them. What's our motto? We do crazy if crazy pays.

And so it was that the Bergens and their attorneys found themselves in The Domestic Relations Division of the Clerk of the Circuit Court of Cook County, The Honorable George Garland presiding.

"I have read the motions by both parties," Garland began. "I am going to give each of you the opportunity to explain your reasoning, after which I trust the matter can be quickly resolved. You may remain at counsel table to respond, and remember, you are under oath."

He turned to Robyn's table. "Mrs. Bergen. Please tell me in your own words why you should have the saddle."

Mary Ann rose.

"Well, your honor. We have already agreed that I would take custody of our horse, Rainbow, and it seems logical that I should also keep the saddle. But more than that, riding on that saddle represents the best of times for me in these recent hard years, and I want those good times to continue more than anything."

"Mr. Bergen?"

"Have you ever ridden a horse, your honor? I hadn't. But in the last year, I feel like I became a real man riding on that saddle. I want it so it can be a touchstone for me as I enter this new chapter in my life."

"Your reasons are very good, and very similar," Garland said. "I anticipated just such a scenario, so I decided to bring in a neutral third party to help me decide. Ask the witness to come in."

Security officers at the back of the courtroom held open the double doors, and a sun-bronzed Adonis—John Wayne 2.0 incarnate—strode down the center aisle. His arm muscles rippled from the weight of the saddle he was carrying, but he showed no sign of strain or exertion. He set it on the floor in front of the bench.

Mary Ann stiffened and turned to Robyn. "What's he doing here?"

Robyn shrugged and looked to opposing counsel's table, where John, similarly shaken, seemed to be asking his attorney the same question.

"Please take the stand," Garland instructed. The witness complied.

He was sworn in and asked to state his name and occupation.

"Eduardo Munoz. I am the stablemaster at the Bergen estate."

"Mr. Munoz. As you know, both Mr. and Mrs. Bergen are claiming ownership of the saddle we see before us. I would like to get your opinion on which of them you think should have it."

Munoz looked at Mary Ann and then at John before turning to the judge.

"Honestly, your honor, they both have done amazing things on that saddle." He turned again to Mary Ann, giving her a sly smile, before turning to John and winking.

"I really don't think I could choose between the two of them."

The couple's confusion instantly turned to rage.

"Both of us?" screamed Mary Ann, jumping up. "You were screwing both of us?"

John was a cheetah, crossing the well of the courtroom to lunge at Munoz, with Mary Ann close behind. Together they yanked him out of the witness box and all three fell to the floor, creating a strange tableau next to the coveted saddle.

Robin and her counterpart entered the fray as the trio got to their feet and John picked up the saddle.

"You can have this worthless piece of shit," he shouted, throwing it. Mary Ann ducked just in time for it to smack Robyn in the face and knock her to the floor.

"Keep it," Mary Ann yelled back. "You two queers deserve it—and each other."

Although it seemed an eternity, the couple was quickly subdued. The judge declared court adjourned pending charges, and as Robyn gathered her papers, she saw John and Mary Ann led away in handcuffs while Munoz talked to the clerk.

***

"Knock, knock." Robyn looked up. "Rough day at the office, dear?"

Robyn gave her fellow attorney the Reader's Digest version of the day's insanity. The intercom buzzed.

"Mary Ann Bergen on line one." Robyn picked up.

"Hi, Mary Ann. What's happening?" As she listened, her expression went from curious to incredulous.

"Okay then. I'll file the paperwork right away. You take care too." She hung up and looked at her coworker.

"The Bergens aren't getting divorced. Apparently, Eduardo Munoz bailed them both out. They talked and decided they could come to an 'arrangement' they all could live with."

"Wow. Who says you shouldn't bet a trifecta?"

Robyn smiled. "Technically, that's a trio bet, not a trifecta."

"What's the difference?"

"In a trifecta, you predict the order in which all three are going to come." She smiled again. "I mean, come in."

~ The Prompt ~

Category:
Flash Fiction

Genre:
Comedy

Location:
Courtroom

Object:
Saddle

Physician, Steel Thyself

Dr. Sherwood had grim news to bear.

This was not unchartered territory for him. In his line of work, he had mastered suppression of his emotions—and even tears—when telling parents of their child's terminal diagnosis.

He picked up the report and read it again. Could he have missed something? Was there any hope? Experimental surgery or alternative medicine? Anything?

But just as the other dozen times he had reviewed the results, the answer was the same.

He set down the report and wiped his eyes. He didn't think he would get through this with his usual composure.

It didn't matter. He had no choice.

He turned off the car, got out, and walked to the house.

His wife was in the kitchen and greeted him with a broad smile.

"Hi, honey," she said, planting a tender kiss on his cheek.

Simultaneously, Dr. Sherwood felt the familiar embrace of four-year-old arms wrapped around his legs.

The group hug over, Mrs. Sherwood started back toward the stove but stopped abruptly and turned in anticipation.

"Oh, I almost forgot," she asked. "Did Ryan's test results come back today like you expected?"

~ The Prompt ~

Free writing exercise using the first sentence:
Dr. Sherwood had grim news to bear.

SMV Seeks SFV (No Weirdos)

Errol Flynn held Olivia de Haviland in a classic swashbuckler's embrace and, clutching his love beads, Eligio felt the familiar flush rise on his cheeks. Even he couldn't say whether it was arousal, or embarrassment for peeking in on their intimacy, but he knew one thing for sure.

Yeah, Baby! Captain Blood was a chick magnet! But who wouldn't be with a name like that?

Eligio turned off the television and checked his phone, again. Nothing. He rose from the modular sectional, padded through the thick, gold shag carpet, and stepped up and out of the conversation pit.

Will this cool bachelor pad ever need to make room for a coffin built for two?

He brushed an errant piece of lint from his red velvet smoking jacket and opened the reverse-engineered wine fridge that kept his favorite libations at a perfect 98.6 degrees.

What type is good for rejection? Eeny, meeny, miny, O!

"Fruit of the Vein" won out over "A Touch of the Nape" and he poured a generous goblet, pondering where his experiment had failed.

I thought it was imminently pragmatic to try online dating. Seemed better than what we did in the 1400s. All that horrid neck biting. Those barbaric castles. Positively primeval.

It took some time for him to find just the right site. Tinder and Match? They sounded a little too interested in fire. Stake Your Claim? Uh-uh. And *Silver* Singles was out of the question. He ultimately signed up for Eternally Yours.

A site named after my life expectancy must be good karma.

But no one had bitten.

Eligio's phone pinged with a message from Eternally Yours: "Remember to check feedback from visitors to your profile."

Maybe this will give me a clue.

He read dozens of entries, each essentially saying the same thing: "Sorry, I haven't got time for anyone who doesn't include a picture."

He raised his red-dagger-fingernailed hand and smacked his forehead.

Curses! Vampires don't show up in photographs.

He sighed in defeat.

Looks like it's back to just necking for me.

~ The Prompt ~

Category:
Nanofiction

Genre:
Failed Experiment

Character:
Eccentric Vampire

Word:
Pragmatic

Revenge is a Dish Best Served Cold

After what happened last Christmas, I didn't think I'd ever see my parents talking to the Brewsters again. But there they are. Geez, Mom and Mrs. Brewster are even hugging. I don't really understand, but when you're eight years old, there's a lot of grown-up stuff that doesn't make sense.

Maybe when you've been neighbors and best friends since you all moved in, it's harder to stay mad. Maybe grown-ups have different rules than kids. All I know is when Lauren Griffith told Jacob that I liked him, and then it got around to the table of popular girls, and they all mocked me in front of everyone in the cafeteria, that's all it took for her to not be my best friend anymore. And we had been friends since first grade!

Of course, Mom and Dad and the Brewsters go back even farther than that. Mom said they met when they both stopped one day to look at their houses being built right next to each other. Jeffrey, my dopey older brother, was three then, just like Travis Brewster. Mom says they watched the boys play in the construction site mud and knew she and Mrs. Brewster would be friends for life.

I was born three years after they moved in, and by that time there were a lot of other houses. Most of the families were also moms and dads with little kids, so it was kind of like a special club. We would play at each other's houses and have sleepovers. The moms and dads would have barbecues and every summer there would be a big block party for what they called the original eight. I don't understand that either, since there were a lot more than eight of us, but like I said, grown-ups don't make a lot of sense.

One thing grown-ups have in common with kids, though, is that when you are really good friends you love to play tricks on each other. Like one summer Dad snuck into the Olsons' back yard and put rubber snakes under the pool cover right before Mr. Olson was going to open the pool for the summer. Dad said Mr. Olson screamed like a little girl, but I think it was a lot louder.

Mr. Olson told dad, "Just you wait, Eddie. I'm going to get you good when you least expect it." Dad drove around for a whole week before he realized Mr. Olson had put a bumper sticker on his car that said, "I wear women's underwear and am proud of it!" Mom laughed and said he *did* get Dad good!

But the best and most fun of all were the Christmas pranks. Everybody always tried to top everybody else. One year Mrs. Gaynor, who mom said was an electrical engineer (I always thought engineers all worked on trains, but I guess not) went around and put a special switch on everyone's outside lights so they were on some kind of timer. Suddenly, the lights would go off on one house, but work on the others. Then it would happen to someone else's house. Everyone thought they were going nuts until Mrs. Gaynor confessed at the New Year's Eve party.

Then came last year, when we had a ton of snow, and the Brewsters made ten big snowmen in their front yard. A few days later, Mrs. Brewster's Bible study group—including the pastor's wife—came to the house. Mrs. Brewster said some of them were smiling, and others just looked funny as they came in. That afternoon, when she went to the grocery store, she saw why. They didn't know that Dad had gone out the night before and moved the carrot noses from the top of the snowman down to where they looked like, well, you know. Dad sent pictures to the neighborhood chat, so Mr. and Mrs. Brewster knew it was him. Everyone thought it was funny, and Mr. Brewster knew it would take a really good prank to get even.

That night, he and Travis waited until everyone was in bed, and they moved all ten of the snowmen to in front of our garage door, on the side where Dad parks. Then they got buckets of water to pour around the bottoms of the snowmen, so they would be frozen stuck to the driveway with ice all around them.

In the morning, Dad got in his car and opened the garage door, but could hardly see behind him. His phone dinged, and it was a picture to the neighborhood chat of what was outside. Mom got the same message, so we bundled up to go outside and look.

While Mom and Dad were in the garage, trying to figure out what to do, I went to get a closer look. I slipped on the ice, hit my head, and was knocked out. So, I didn't cry or make any noise. That's when Dad decided he could just hit the gas hard and barrel through the snowmen.

He was right, and that's why all the neighbors, including the Brewsters, are standing around crying at Murphy's Funeral Home with me lying in a casket.

If anybody gets this message, tell Lauren Griffith I'm not mad anymore. I guess if Mom and Dad aren't holding a grudge, I really shouldn't either.

~ The Prompt ~

Category: Short Story

Story much touch on the following topic in some way:

It was a cozy neighborhood where everybody knew everyone else and there was never a shortage of people to help when one was in need. There was also a lot of tomfoolery going on, which he and his wife had always enjoyed, until now. The winter snowman practical jokes had been funny over the years but, this time, their neighbor had taken it way too far...

The Rainbow of War: Olive Drab, Silver Bracelets, Yellow Ribbons

Southeast Asia – November 1972

"Kevin L. Perner. Corporal, United States Army. 537-18-6249."

Captain Lê Văn Bảo sighs deeply and gives a nearly imperceptible nod. The crack from the steel pipe swung by the junior officer into the prisoner's kneecap can be heard throughout the filthy jungle compound.

Corporal Perner begins to buckle but is forced back to standing.

"Is this getting tiresome for you, Corporal?" Captain Bảo asks. "We can stop as soon as you answer my question. How many men came ashore with you last night?"

"Kevin L. Perner. Corporal, United States Army. 537-18-6249."

"Enough!" Captain Bảo screams. He gestures to his subordinate, who begins striking the prisoner everywhere with the pipe.

Corporal Perner drops to the fetal position. He writhes and howls in agony, cries of pain jumbled with his name, rank, and serial number.

"Stop...Kevin L. Perner... 537... don't kill me... Corporal... my leg... United Stated Army... 6 249... my leg... my leg... Kevin L. Perner... Kevin... Corporal...Kevin... Kevin..."

"Kevin. Kevin. It's okay. Kevin, wake up."

Someone is shaking him. Kevin opens his eyes. Nurse Donna Newmark, almost nose-to-nose with him, has him in a bear hug in his hospital bed. She smiles.

"I thought you were going to fling yourself into next week," she says. "You were really thrashing this time. One of the bad ones, huh?"

"They're all bad." *Just like everything in my shitty life.*

"It seems like they're happening less often, so that's good." Donna works the crank on the end of the bed to sit Kevin up. "And it's a beautiful morning. Ready for breakfast?"

Jesus H. Christ. All the fucking nurses in the army and I had to get Little Mary Sunshine.

"I'm not hungry. But I gotta pee. Where's the goddamn pee bottle? And my cigarettes?"

Donna pulls over the side table that holds the bedside urinal and Kevin's cigarettes.

"I'll be back for that in a few minutes. I'll bring you some coffee and see if you've changed your mind about breakfast." She pulls the privacy curtain around the bed and leaves.

Kevin lights a cigarette, grabs the bottle, and pulls back the covers. As he relieves himself, he stares at the empty spot on the bed where the bottom half of his leg should be.

Crystal Lake, Illinois – October 1971

Linda Dobecki drops her books and plops onto the twin bed. Donny Osmond smiles down at her from the countless pictures her younger sister, Karen, has plastered on the walls on her side of the room. Linda rolls her eyes and flips onto her belly.

Oh my God. So childish. Doesn't she know there's more important things happening than stupid teeny bopper singers?

She reaches into the book bag and pulls out the mimeographed flyer from the assembly. Linda was mesmerized by the speaker, a senior from the University of Illinois named Gail representing VIVA—Voices in Vital America. She talked about the soldiers in Vietnam who were missing in action. No one knew if they were lost, dead, or captured, but college students didn't want them to be forgotten. So, VIVA started making and selling bracelets with their name, rank, branch, and the date they went missing.

Of course, Linda knew about the war, but it wasn't something real to her. It was just noise on the news to her.

Until today.

Gail's stories and slides were a master class in the horrors of war, and Linda – MIA/POW bracelet firmly affixed to her wrist—walked away determined to make a difference.

The flyer says that students can write to their soldier care of an address in Washington. Linda grabs a multicolored pad of letter-writing paper from her nightstand and begins.

October 15, 1971

Dear Kevin,

My name is Linda Dobecki and I'm a junior at Crystal Lake HS in Crystal Lake, Illinois. I don't know if you know about the MIA/POW bracelets (that stands for Missing in Action and Prisoner of War), but I got one today and your name was on it. It says you went missing on September 7, 1971. That was our first day of school this year, so I feel like it was a sign or something.

I learned a lot about the war today and about how bad you guys have it. I thought even though there isn't a lot I can do from here, at least I can write and let you know that someone is thinking about you. Anyway, I don't know if you'll ever get this letter, but then I thought even if you don't, maybe you'll feel some good vibes knowing that someone back home is thinking about you, which I PROMISE I will do every day!

I also PROMISE I'll send a letter every week until you are home. I'm not sure what I'll write about. Probably boring stuff like school, and my dumb sister, and other stuff, but if this gets to you, maybe it will help you forget about the war for a minute and think about home.

Well, I'll stop now so I have something to write next week. Don't forget that there are a lot of people thinking about you guys and waiting for your return. I hope you are in a really good hiding place and not captured! Stay safe, peace and love!

Your friend,

Linda

Camp Zama Army Hospital, Japan – December 1972

Kevin sits in his wheelchair in the sharing circle, smoking and looking down at the floor. He wants no part of it.

These crybabies. What do they think? If they "open up" about their feelings, there's going to be a goddamn bolt of lightning and they'll walk again? They're gonna sprout an arm where the commies blew off the old one? Their girlfriends won't care they can't get it up anymore, or they're missing their fucking ear. It's bullshit.

"Thank you, Phil," the moderator says. "Who wants to share next? How about you, Kevin?"

"I don't want to fucking share," Kevin spits. "This is bullshit."

"Even if it doesn't help you, your story may help another vet."

Kevin throws down his cigarette butt and crushes it with his remaining foot.

"Okay," he yells. "Sure. Let's see how many people I can convert with my touching story. I got captured by the Cong. They put us in shacks in the jungle like animals.

"The pinko captain in charge of us musta seen a lot of World War Two movies, because he had torture down to a science. He'd take us one at a time for questioning and beat the shit of us until we couldn't talk anymore. But I never cracked. Name, rank, and serial number, that's all I gave the prick.

"Guess what he got in return? My leg. I went in there with two legs, but he musta wanted to end my big dancing career, because every time he beat me—wait, that's wrong—he had a lackey to beat me—he just watched. Musta got off on it or something. Anyway, anytime the lackey beat me, he started with my knee. Beat me everywhere else, too, but beat the living shit out of my knee. I'd get dragged back to my cell and could see pieces of the kneecap through the hole there.

"I shouldn't complain, though. After it got infected, it gave me something to look at. The red line moving down my leg, and the maggots swimming around in the wound. But here's the inspiring part—listen close, fellas. I'm one of the lucky ones, because they liberated us before the infection spread to the rest of my body. All they had to do was cut off my leg. I'm sooo lucky. Just my leg. Brings a tear to your eye, don't it? Who else wants to share and inspire everybody?"

Kevin lights another cigarette and wheels himself out of the room.

Crystal Lake, Illinois – December 1971 – March 1973

December 1, 1971

Dear Kevin,

I so hope you've been getting my letters! I know it's always hot in Vietnam, but here in Illinois we've had a bunch of snow and it's COLD. I bet that would feel great to you. Oh, I hope it doesn't make you feel bad or jealous me saying that.

Anyway, I wanted to send you something for Christmas that I hope will be a good luck charm. We had a field trip to the Museum of Science and Industry (that's in Chicago), and there was this display about amber. Do you know what that is? I didn't. Turns out trees release resin (kind of like sap, but not really) to protect their bark. It's sticky, and sometimes bugs or other things get stuck in it, and then the resin kind of closes around it and hardens. It makes a fossil. Some people are lucky enough to find them in the wild, but I found mine in the museum gift shop (ha ha). I thought if something could survive maybe for millions of years, it could help you survive and find your way back home. Stay safe, peace and love, and Merry Christmas!

Your friend,

Linda

April 19, 1972

Dear Kevin,

Jerry Nickols asked me to prom today!!! I've had a secret crush on him for a long time (and I mean SECRET—DON'T TELL ANYBODY!), and I was afraid he didn't even know I was alive, and I don't know if my best friend said something, but it doesn't matter anyway because HE ASKED ME TO PROM TODAY!

Okay, I would write more, but I'm so excited I can't think of anything else. Plus, now my mom and I are going shopping to look for dresses. I know this isn't probably the most important news from home, but I wanted you to be the first to know!

Did you go to prom before you went into the Army? I better go now. Stay safe, peace and love!

Your friend,

Linda Nickols (ha ha wishful thinking!)

July 9, 1972

Dear Kevin,

Not much room on this postcard. Hi from Wisconsin Dells where we're on vacation. REALLY wish you were here.

Peace & love,

Linda

September 7, 1972

Dear Kevin,

Oh my God, I just realized it's been one year since you've been missing. Every night I say a prayer that you are OK and are somehow getting my letters.

Anway, school started two days ago and I'm a SENIOR!!! Jerry and I are still dating and we're going to homecoming later this month. Gosh, I wish I could talk to you and learn about when you were in school. Because you are doing such grown up things like being in the army and in a war, I feel like you are so much older than me, but probably not.

Well, my nasty English teacher gave us tons of homework, even though it's the first week of school, so I have to go and get it done. Stay safe, peace and love!

Your friend,

Linda

December 5, 1972

Dear Kevin,

Like it says on the front of this card, there's no place like home for Christmas. I hope you get home soon.

Peace and love,

Linda

March 1, 1973

Dear Kevin,

The school year is flying by so fast! But that's not what I want to tell you about today. I don't know what news you hear from home, but there's a new song out about somebody in prison and when he comes home his girlfriend has a yellow ribbon tied around the tree to show she wants him back. But guess what! Everyone here is wearing yellow ribbons and tying them around trees, and it's not because we have boyfriends in prison (ha ha). It's to show how much we want the soldiers from Vietnam to come home! Anyway, I'm sending a yellow ribbon to you so you can imagine them all over the place! I hope that makes you feel better, wherever you are.

Peace and love,
Linda

Camp Zama Army Hospital, Japan – April 1973

Sweat rolls down Kevin's face and back as he propels himself between the parallel bars. It's his third physical therapy session using his prosthetic leg, and cheerleader Donna is at his side.

"You're doing great, Kevin! No, don't depend so much on your right leg. I know it's tough, but you've gotta put weight on the new one. Once you master it, you'll be sent stateside to finish rehab in a VA hospital there!"

"It's not a fucking leg!" he yells. "It's a torture device. It's not worth all this. Give me the goddamn wheelchair. I'm done."

What's the use? I'm gonna be a lousy cripple when I get home with or without some magic fake leg. This is bullshit. Why didn't that pinko captain just finish me off?

"Maybe it is a good time for a break," Donna says. "We'll work more later."

She pushes Kevin into his ward. A large pouch with Red Cross markings sits on his bed. Donna smiles.

"Looks like mail call finally caught up to you!" She moves the pouch to the side table and helps Kevin get into bed.

Kevin undoes the string on the pouch's flap and upends the contents onto his lap. More than a hundred pastel envelopes, covered in peace symbols and flowers, cascade across the blanket. An equally flowery handwriting in purple ink reveals the sender to be one Linda Dobecki of Crystal Lake, Illinois.

Kevin plucks a small package from the pile and opens it first. The sterile glare of the institutional fluorescent bulbs softens as it passes through the golden amber, and for possibly the first time since his arrival at Camp Zama, Corporal Kevin L. Perner smiles.

Crystal Lake, Illinois – June 3, 1973

"Dad, wait! Don't take the picture. I forgot something."

Linda retrieves the yellow ribbon from her bedroom and pins it to her graduation robe; it appears luminescent against the black fabric. She positions her sleeve to ensure the metal bracelet is visible.

"Okay, I'm ready. And remember, take two so I can put one in my letter to Kevin."

"Yes, sir!" her father answers, snapping two shots with the Polaroid camera.

"We'd better get moving," her mom chimes in. "I don't want to have to climb to the top of the bleachers!"

Downey VA Hospital, North Chicago, Illinois – June 3, 1973

Corporal Kevin L. Perner stands in front of the full-length mirror. He tugs at his left pant leg so it falls naturally over the prosthesis and pats his jacket pocket to make sure the envelope and small box are inside.

"The car is ready, Corporal." A private stands in the doorway.

"I'm ready." Kevin grabs his garrison cap and cane and follows the private to the elevator.

Crystal Lake, Illinois – June 3, 1973

The station wagon pulls into the driveway late that afternoon. After sitting in the hot sun for three hours, and then stuffing themselves at the Sizzler, there is a lot less spring in everyone's step as they shuffle back toward the house. No one notices the idling olive drab sedan pull away from the curb a few houses down the block.

"What's this?" Karen says, picking up a small, wrapped package with an envelope attached. "Oh. It's for Linda."

"More recognition for the graduate, no doubt," Linda says, taking the items from her disappointed sister.

"Go blow," says her sister as she follows their parents into the house.

Linda gasps at the envelope's return address. She goes inside and heads for her room.

"Anybody want some iced tea?" her mom asks.

"I'll be down in a few minutes, Mom. I'm going to change my clothes."

Linda shuts her bedroom door and sits on her bed, staring at the envelope.

Is it from him, or is it from someone telling me he's dead? Dear God, please let him be alive.

She unseals the envelope and begins to read.

June 2, 1973

Dear Linda,

It's my turn to be the letter writer after all the letters you sent me. You kept apologizing for them being boring or silly, but let me tell you one thing, and I'm not going to beat around the bush. Your letters saved my life.

I'm not exaggerating. I was in a prison camp for just over a year. It was hell, and when we were liberated, I got sent to an Army hospital in Japan. They had to cut off my leg. I was so angry, I really wished I'd been killed instead of saved. Everyone tried to help, but I didn't care. I didn't cooperate. I just wanted everyone to leave me alone so I could die. Honestly, it was just a matter of time before I took care of it myself.

Then, two months ago, I got a package, filled with all your letters. Your kind, funny, silly, letters. On flower power stationery in purple ink. Full of peace and love, just like you always signed off. You didn't know if they'd get to me, but you kept writing. Remember that good vibe you hoped I'd feel? I think maybe that's what kept me alive until your letters came. Anyway (as you would say, ha ha), you didn't give up on me, so I decided I couldn't give up on myself. I finally buckled down, and last month I got transferred to the States to finish rehab. I asked to be sent to Illinois. Thankfully, I was.

I hope we can meet in person soon. I didn't want to intrude on your big day today, but I did want to say congratulations and thank you and drop off a little gift. I made it in one of my occupational therapy classes in rehab. I hope it brings you all the luck it did for me. And lots of peace and love.

Your friend,

Kevin

Linda realizes the paper is wet with her tears. She wipes them away and sets down the letter. She unties the bow on the small box, lifts the lid, and unfolds tissue paper.

The piece of amber she sent Kevin for Christmas has been set into a delicate metal framework, with a small loop at the top so it can be worn as a necklace. Instead of a chain, a long yellow ribbon is threaded through the loop.

Linda ties the ribbon around her neck, grabs her flower power stationery and purple pen.

June 3, 1973

Dear Kevin,

Oh my God, you're alive! I KNEW you would …

~ The Prompt ~

Category: Short story
Character: An amputee
Setting: A rehabilitation center
Must include: A piece of amber with something related to or derived from living matter preserved in it

Silence is Golden or Strange Strangers on a Train

Randy had endured judgment and harassment his whole life. He finally learned the best way to deal with it was to turn a deaf ear.

Randy looked up from his phone as the train rumbled into the station. He pocketed the phone and lifted the handle on his rolling bag as it slowed. Tall and lean, with sharp features and close-cropped blond hair ("a crew cut with a little swagger," he instructed his stylist), he never failed to turn heads wherever he went. Even if he couldn't hear their comments, he certainly noticed the attention. *Fifty-five may not be the new thirty-five, but close enough.*

Randy walked through the coach car, grateful he had splurged on a business class seat for the three-hour ride to Des Moines. He could see one baby already crying and while that in and of itself didn't bother him, he knew it wouldn't be long before you could cut the tension with a knife in the cheap seats.

His decision was further validated when he reached his seat. Unlike the worn vinyl found in coach, this was lushy-padded fabric in a shade of blue reminiscent of his Mediterranean vacation. Such memories would be a welcome distraction from the sepia-toned silent movie of flatlands playing on a continuous loop out his window.

While others plugged in their earbuds, Randy grabbed the hefty, multi-sectioned Sunday newspaper from the outer pocket before stowing his bag overhead. For him, reading meant holding the physical material in his hand—although his finally acquiesced a few years ago to include e-books in that credo. He leaned back and hoped for a peaceful journey before the chaos that would greet him upon arrival.

His tranquility—as well as any hope for it continuing—was shattered two stops later as another passenger came barreling into the seat across from him, nearly tearing the opened newspaper in two as the second of his three bags (*Wasn't there a two-bag limit?*) swung from his arm and hit it.

Randy looked him straight in the eye.

"Sorry, pal," the guy said. "I've been hauling ass to make this train, and then the dipwad conductor has me get on at the all the freakin' way at the other end. I had to push though loads of idiots to get here."

Randy smiled and raised his hand as if to say, "no worries," and lifted his newspaper, hoping New Guy would understand the universal sign for "I don't want to talk."

Pretending to read, Randy kept one eye on New Guy, whose monologue about lazy idiots and rip-offs and his rights never waned as he shoved his oversized bags into the compartment, finally having to leave one on the floor, intruding on both of their leg space.

The conductor, whose nametag read "Edward," appeared. After checking New Guy's ticket, he turned to Randy.

"Back to Des Moines, huh Randy," he said, "You must be a glutton for punishment."

He smiled, nodded, and gave the conductor a "what can I say?" shrug. Edward gave his shoulder a pat and moved on to the next passengers.

Randy went back to his newspaper, this time intending to read for real, but New Guy's flailing-armed outburst caught his attention.

"Can you believe this B.S.?" New Guy railed, pointing at the front page of Randy's newspaper. "A bunch of faggot drag queens are going to put on a show in downtown Des Moines! I thought we were safe from this homo crap in Iowa."

Randy sat quietly and just watched as the rant continued.

"My damn father would be rolling in his grave if he knew this was happening," New Guy continued. "Somebody has to put these pansies in their place. Damn, I wish I wasn't on my way to a big meeting—the morons at my company can't get anything done without me, so I can't miss it. Boy, if I could though, I'd take one of those queer assholes out back and give him—if you can even call him a *him*—what for. Faggots! In Des Moines!"

As tempting as it was for Randy to respond, his watch vibrated just as an announcement came over the loudspeaker that they would be arriving in Des Moines in thirty minutes. Without comment, Randy stood, retrieved his bag from the overhead bin, and walked to the restroom.

Twenty-five minutes later, New Guy was still shaking his head and muttering to himself when the statuesque redhead appeared in the aisle next to his seat. The beautiful creature was wearing a lowcut, skintight pink cocktail dress, complemented by fishnet stockings and—in deference to the Iowa chill—an elaborate, multi-colored, knee-length cloak that would have made New Guy think of *Joseph and the Amazing Technicolor Dreamcoat* if he'd ever once set foot in anything akin to a theatre.

New Guy first saw the feet, clad in five-inch pink stilettos, making the redhead almost seven feet tall. His smile got bigger and more lascivious as his eyes slowly made their way up past the fishnets and clingy dress. It was only when he got to the face that he stopped short.

New Guy sat, bug-eyed and mouth agape, *finally* at a loss for words. Randy winked and gave him a fluttery hand wave and million-dollar smile. *Darn it. I must remember to have my camera ready next time.*

The conductor tapped Randy on his shoulder, knowing they would have to be face-to-face so Randy could read his lips.

"Looks like there is quite a crowd already at the station—supporters and protestors," he said. "I hope you're ready for it."

"Nothing we haven't seen before, Edward," Randy replied, his decibel level and distinctive deaf accent turning a few heads in Business Class, including New Guy's.

"Besides, it's going to be a piece of cake after the ride I've had," he added, looking straight at New Guy before turning back to the conductor.

"You know, Edward, sometimes it's really a blessing to be deaf."

~ The Prompt ~

Category:
Short Story

Photo Prompt:
The view out the window from a luxurious train car

Character:
A tall deaf person past middle age, with very short hair, wearing high heels and an elaborate, brightly colored, knee-length coat.

And Sew it Goes

Sometimes you only need to pull one thread to make everything unravel.

Charlene was a model employee at Designer Prep International. Every morning, while most of her two hundred coworkers were chatting and still getting settled, her machine was humming at eight on the dot as she sewed the preliminary pieces that would be sent for final assembly to clothing manufacturers around the world.

Per the company manual, which Charlene had memorized by her second day on the job, her work area was free of personal items, food, and drink; her scissors, tape measure, and other work tools set positioned exactly as designated on the diagram in the manual.

As coworkers risked reprimand for idle chatter and trips to the bathroom outside of their allocated fifteen-minute break, Charlene loved the precise schedule, instructions, and expectations. Following them made her a perfect employee, and Charlene loved perfection.

On her first day, a few women invited her to sit with them at lunch. Before sitting, she pulled a disinfectant wipe from her bag and cleaned both the seat and the table. The next day, the table had no room for her.

It was all the same to Charlene, who hadn't enjoyed listening to them complain about being unappreciated automatons trapped in a sweat shop. How could they feel that way? She knew she had found her ideal job for life: a place where her sense of organization and policy compliance would be appreciated and recognized.

It also was nothing new to her. Any friends she thought she'd made in school vanished when the teacher made an example of her attention to detail on projects or her orderly desk. She ate alone in those lunchrooms too, organizing her M&Ms by color to block out the teasing.

And so it went, for twenty-five years. Each morning, Charlene arrived in time to stow her things in her equally organized locker, don her apron, clean and straighten her work area as needed after the third shift, and got to work. She ignored the eye rolling and whispers of her coworkers and took satisfaction in doing a superior job to each and every one of them.

***

The alarm went off at five a.m. As always, Charlene did not allow herself the luxury of emptying her bladder until her bed was made with meticulous precision. She then proceeded through her rigid morning routine, which culminated in packing her lunch for the day. Knowing what a monumental day this would be, she deviated from her normal menu and added a cupcake as a special treat.

Charlene took a walk through the apartment, making sure all was in order. Today of all days, it needed to be perfect. She picked up her purse and lunch bag and walked out.

The bag containing the AR-15 was already in the trunk of her car.

***

Homicide Detective James Streit brought the survivors into the lunchroom for questioning. Most of them were women, and nearly all were sobbing. A middle-aged redhead went first.

"It all happened so fast," she said. "Everyone who got their break at 10:15 had gotten up, including Charlene. She usually got up, went to the bathroom, and then went right back to her machine. She didn't go outside to smoke, or stand around and talk, or get a snack. She was always back and ready to work before anybody else.

"At first, it seemed normal. But then she went to her locker. When she came out, she had a big bag with her, and something else in her other hand. She set that down on a chair and just stood at the front of the room while everybody got back to their machines.

"Then, calm as anything, she opened the bag, pulled out a big gun, and just started shooting back and forth. Luckily, I saw her take the gun out and was able to duck before she got to my side of the room. Everyone was screaming and the noise from the gun was terrible—worse than anything I've ever seen in a movie.

"Then, as fast as it started, it stopped. I thought maybe she ran out of bullets. I peeked up to see if she was reloading, but she had set down the gun, and then I saw what the other thing was—a cupcake! And she was just sitting on a chair eating it. Like nothing had happened."

"What happened next?" Streit asked. A gray-haired woman of about sixty took over.

"At first, everybody froze. Who knew if she was gonna pick the gun back up to get the rest of us. But she just sat there eating the cupcake.

"Some of the people who were shot were still alive so we went to them. Someone called 911. By that time, the supervisor came in. He must have heard the noise."

"What about the shooter?"

"She just sat there," the gray-haired woman continued. "Larry—that's the supervisor—said something to her like, 'It's okay, Cheryl. The police are on their way. Don't move and no one is going to hurt you.'"

"Cheryl?" Streit asked. "I thought her name was Charlene."

"Yeah, Larry's a dick. He doesn't know anybody's name. I'm surprised he even talked to her. I guess he wanted to make sure his own sorry ass was safe."

"Okay, so what did she do?"

"Nothing. She just looked at him all calm and said, 'I'm done. Don't worry about me.' She had finished the stupid cupcake, so she just sat with her hands folded in her lap like she was waiting for a bus or something. Then you guys and the paramedics got here and you know the rest."

The detective thanked the employees and asked them to stay in the lunchroom. He went through the factory floor and into the supervisor's office, where Charlene was seated on a chair, her hands and feet shackled.

"Did you Miranda her?" he asked.

"Yes, sir," a young uniform answered.

"I'll take over from here."

The detective pulled up a chair in front of Charlene.

"Charlene—may I call you Charlene?"

She nodded.

Charlene, I'm Detective Streit. I'd like to ask you some questions."

She just stared ahead.

"Why did you do this today?"

"I don't really feel like going through it all again."

"What do you mean? Who has spoken to you?"

"No one," she answered. "But I know you probably already have a warrant to search my apartment. It's all there. And in good order. You won't have any problems. Now, are you going to take me to jail?"

***

The apartment manager opened the door to Charlene's apartment; Streit and his team went in.

"They said she was a clean freak, but holy shit," one of the men said. "It's like a model home."

"Hopefully that will make it easier," Streit said. "Let's take a look around."

There was nothing out of the ordinary in Charlene's living room, kitchen, bathroom, or bedroom. The second bedroom, which served as her office, was another story.

Just as neat and tidy as the rest of the apartment, the office was a shrine to her virtual perfectionism. One wall was covered with recognition from her school days: perfect attendance; never tardy; fifth grade spelling bee winner; library assistant.

The opposite wall was covered with a what looked like homemade certificates with strange accomplishments: original seam ripper; no threads left; zero extra pee breaks; spools and bobbins in proper order. Streit was summoned to the desk. He picked up a large, leather-bound book and opened it. Various pages had been flagged with sticky notes marked, "read me."

"It's a journal," Streit said. He read the flagged passages.

July 19, 1999

My first day at Designer Prep International was a dream! I brought home the manual to study, and it's going to be great. They love organization and have a lot of rules, but they are easy to follow. I'm going to fit right in!

August 11, 1999

As usual, it's been hard to make friends at work. But, that's okay. As long as the company recognizes my value, I don't need friends there. Besides, I'm doing so great, I don't think I'll be on the sewing floor for long!

July 20, 2009

I know there are a lot of people that have worked here a long time, but I really thought I'd get some recognition for my 10th anniversary. Maybe this place isn't what I thought it was. I'm upset. Really upset.

May 2, 2013

Oh my God, that idiot Loretta at the machine next to me just got her 5th seam ripper since I've worked here. She lost 2 and wore out or broke the other 3. I have the original one I got and it's right where it's supposed to be in my work area and I've NEVER EVEN USED IT because I sew everything correctly the first time. After 14 years with the company, I think they should recognize that.

December 20, 2019

Wow. A few people actually said "Merry Christmas" to me today at the end of our so-called Christmas party. The "party" consisted of an extra half hour for lunch with stale Christmas cookies and warm, spiked eggnog. Since it took twenty years, I'm guessing it was the eggnog talking.

June 14, 2022

If that JERK Larry calls me "Cheryl" one more time I'm going to lose it. What a useless waste of skin. I'm not worried. He's going to get his someday.

October 10, 2023

What is this, Junior High? Can't anyone clean up after themselves? It's bad enough I have to clean up after the lazy night shift person, but now everyone that sits around me purposely makes sure extra thread and pieces of fabric somehow make it into my area. They know I'm going to clean up every night, so they just make me clean up after them, too. Bitches.

July 19, 2024

Today was my 25th anniversary at DPI. Not so much as a handshake from anyone. Well, I guess it's time to retire. Me, and whoever else I can take with me.

I know the police are reading this, so now you know what made me do it. If you don't want this to keep happening, maybe you should let people know that even sweat shop automatons need a pat on the back every once in a while.

***

Charlene carried her tray to the conveyor belt at the end of the dining room. The attendant smiled and thanked her, which prompted a broad smile in return.

She walked through the locked down mental health facility. Others who were also free to move about played checkers, worked on puzzles, and read. She decided she'd had enough interaction for the day and headed back to her room.

She noticed the throw rug next to the bed was askew. As she felt her face flush, she remembered her anger management techniques and closed her eyes to center herself. After a few deep breaths, she bent down to straighten the rug and sat at her desk, opened her new journal, and wrote.

September 8, 2026

I've been here for 2 years now. If they continue to see me showing progress, I may be released in another 2 or 3. I've listened carefully to what the doctors and therapists say and have learned to look like I'm controlling my anger and emotions.

Every night I pray that when I get out, Larry is still at DPI. "Cheryl" really owes him a visit.

~ The Prompt ~

Category: Short story

Genre: Drama

Theme: Cog in the Machine

Character: Perfectionist

End of the Road

It was the same question each time Marie climbed these front steps.

Will it be Dad in the house, or someone who thinks I'm a stranger?

Marie dropped her purse in the foyer and carried a tin into the den. She and Ellen, the caregiver, said hello. Her father, seemingly one with the faded, green plaid recliner, maintained his trancelike stare out the back window.

"How is he today?"

"Tom's been pretty quiet," Ellen replied, picking up his untouched food tray. "I've tried everything, but today he's obsessed with something outside." She shrugged. "That's just how it is sometimes."

Ellen left the room and Marie began their ritual.

"I have your favorite, Dad, Tootsie Rolls," she enticed, prying open the lid and presenting it with a flourish. Nothing.

Marie helped herself and stood behind the recliner. She closed her eyes and fifty-plus years in their beloved "rec room" produced a virtual—albeit somewhat disheveled—Norman Rockwell exhibition featuring her family. When she opened them, only the final tableau remained, a lonely scene devoid of once-vibrant colors, now dulled by the turpentine known as dementia.

Marie followed her dad's gaze out the window to the object of his obsession.

Of course. The car. His pride and joy. The other woman, Mom used to say.

At the far end of the driveway, the sedan's meticulously polished finish glimmered in the sun like a smooth sheet of ice on wintry pond in January at high noon.

Tom was born with motor oil in his veins and spent forty years as a mechanic. When he retired, he decided it was time for his first brand-new car.

His first, and his last.

"Big Blue is still looking good, huh Dad?" Marie said. He shifted and began struggling to reach something in the crevice between the seat and the arm.

"Let me, Dad," Marie said, taking over. She pulled out a dog-eared, faded picture.

Her mother—tiny, with a blonde ponytail—was posing with her dad's *first* other woman, a 1957 Buick Century.

"That's a great picture of Mom," she began, but the doorbell interrupted. "I'll be right back."

Jim Ulrich was there to pay for and pick up Big Blue.

"My daughter Elyse is so excited, she ran straight to the car," Jim laughed. "When it's your first car…"

Shouting from the den interrupted him, and both hurried toward it.

"It's Joanie! She's by the car!" Tom exclaimed again and again.

Elyse—tiny, with a blonde ponytail—was beaming in front of her new wheels.

Marie turned to correct him and saw the first expression of happiness she'd seen in months.

He beamed, his voice strong with certainty.

"Marie, your mother is here. She loves that car."

He turned back to the window.

"Joanie," he murmured softly. "Joanie."

Marie wiped away tears, bent close and squeezed her dad's shoulders.

"You're right, Dad," she whispered. "Mom loves Big Blue almost as much as she loves you."

~ The Prompt ~

Category:
Flash Fiction

1st sentence:
Must be twelve words

Include:
A second-hand item

Also include:
Five words that end in "ice"

The Malignant Narcissist

A malignant narcissist writes an autobiography to die for. Literally.

I am a blight upon the world. On that we all agree.
But even monsters get to write their own biography.
So here it is, my tale to tell, to set the record straight.
Don't be surprised if on the floor you find the lunch you ate.

For true enough my story's filled with pain and death and gore.
Unlike some storytellers I don't leave them wanting more.

I mark no real beginning; I have been here for all time.
Although my toll is millions, I'm convicted of no crime.
You see, I work in shadows, sometimes found, but never stopped.
Each effort to destroy me has magnificently flopped.

My carnage is of legend, such delicious butchery.
A mixture I have patented of sadist potpourri.

Descriptions, oh so graphic, all begin at Grandma's knee
so children grow up petrified of what they'll someday see.
Because they know my killing isn't just a grown-up game.
No carding people at my door, to me you're all the same.

I cut off limbs, I blind the eye, I cause the brain to rot.
While legions try to stop me I just mock: "That's all you got?"
At times I'm quite inelegant, the work can be a drudge.
If diarrhea does the job, well, who are you to judge?

Of course, some beg for mercy, offer bribes they cannot pay.
I make them think I've changed my mind; come back another day.

And even if I set them free and go against myself
I make them sick with worry—Evil Elf Upon the Shelf.

Now to be fair I really must give credit where it's due,
for oftentimes the help I get is too good to be true.
Despite the warnings everywhere to circumvent my path,
some self-destructive GPS leads many to my wrath.

And then you'd think my advent would at last provoke a fight.
Alas, so many give up, saying, "I don't have the might."
I guess it should embarrass me, this glaring lack of flair,
but later they're still just as dead, so I don't really care.

I've many more examples but I think you get the gist.
Just look around and you will find whatever I have missed.
Besides, you'll know the secrets I am keeping now at bay
when it becomes your own turn and I visit you one day.

Such giddy expectation: I just know that we will click!
Can't wait to get inside you and find out what makes you tick.
Don't worry, nothing's imminent. It's years until I call…
hold on, it might be sooner, since you're lighting that Pall Mall.

Oh dear, where are my manners? My bad breeding is to blame.
I've prattled on and on and never offered up my name.
My given name is Cancer; I have quite the pedigree.
But no need to be formal. You can just call me Big C.

~ The Prompt ~

Category: Rhyming Short Story
Genre: Horror
Theme: Bribery
Emotion: Petrified

On My Last Day (This Call May Be Recorded for Quality Control Purposes)

It's always wise to conduct an exit interview. Otherwise, an employee might find another way to say all the things she wanted to say, "On My Last Day."

Kathy leaned back in her chair and took off the headset and her glasses, rubbing first her eyes and then her sore temples. She then logged off the computer, starting the five-minute countdown to vacate her seat before the next customer service rep swooped in to take it. Any delay in that prisoner swap meant trouble for both.

At least half of that allotment was required to rearrange her workstation back to the needs of the right-handed world. Even when she offered to buy a left-handed mouse with her own money, the by-the-book supervisor pointed out Section 4.3 of the Employee Manual—Official Office Equipment. So, every day just before 7:00 a.m., like a seventh grader's backpack hiding "someone else's" Virginia Slims, Kathy's purse played the Trojan horse. Once safely stowed under her desk, Kathy swapped out the mouse cord for the wireless dongle, concealed the company mouse, and placed its lookalike to the left of her keyboard with the speed and precision of the pit crew at Indy. At 3:00 p.m., the maneuver was repeated in reverse.

She was especially cheerful as she vacated her cubicle this afternoon, her penultimate day on the job. But it was more than retirement that put a spring in Kathy's step. Much more.

When Kathy joined the fledgling Rainforest Peak—the ultimate online shopping site, per its own hype—she was one of a few dozen women who fielded customer service calls in a sincerely helpful manner. Most callers were decent enough, but some were nasty:

CUST: What kind of bullshit company is this that you promise overnight delivery and it takes two days?
REP: I'm very sorry for the inconvenience, sir. I will issue you a full refund for the shipping charge as well as a 15% credit to your account to be used on a future purchase.

CUST: Damn right you will. I don't want to have to talk to your supervisor, little lady.
REP: That won't be necessary, sir. Is there anything else I can help you with today?

And the rest of them were just plain idiots:

CUST: I got this new phone, but the charger doesn't work.
REP: I'm very sorry, ma'am. Please tell me a little more.

CUST: So, I plugged the cord into the phone, and then I plugged the other end into that square thing, but nothing's happening. The phone is still dead.
REP: Have you made sure the outlet is working properly?

CUST: What outlet?
REP: The outlet where you plugged in the charging block, the, uh, "square thing."
CUST: That has to get plugged in somewhere too?

It didn't take the "little ladies" long to come up with a great way to channel the aggravation caused by roughly half their calls without turning their tongues into bloody stumps in the process. They started a call log, separate and secret from the official one. They named it, "On My Last Day."

Into this log went all the things they *wanted* to say to the obnoxious, idiotic, chauvinistic, belittling customers, but couldn't:

- "Hey, Thomas Edison. They got this new thing now called electricity. You should try it sometime."
- "You want to return that diet plan you bought that doesn't work? Here's an idea. Why don't you return the ice cream maker and case of brownie mix that was in the same order. That might help."
- "Hey, asshole. I'm not your 'little lady,' but God help whoever is. She must've drowned puppies in another life to get stuck with you in this one."

But Kathy added the ultimate retort, which became not only everyone's favorite, but the go-to phrase when just nothing else would do:

- "Are you FUCKING kidding me?"

It was so popular, in fact, that Kathy gave all the gals handmade ornaments that Christmas, with "AYFKM?" embroidered in cheery red and green. None made it home but instead hung in a discrete place of honor in each woman's cubicle.

So, despite the challenge of dealing with difficult people all day long, Kathy and her colleagues loved coming to work, trading war stories over lunch, and adding snarky retorts to their burgeoning literary endeavor.

That is, until Rainforest Peak started swallowing up other companies and monopolized the online shopping world. This led to a change in corporate management, which eventually trickled down to the call center. Their beloved supervisor was let go and replaced by a cocky, butt-licking blowhard who never worked in customer service a day in his life. His first order of business was to fix what wasn't broken.

Overnight, the chatty, conversational interactions with customers were eliminated. Marketing experts drafted strict scripts for the women to use, with severe penalties for any deviations. And they were reminded at the start of each call that big brother most assuredly was listening:

"This call may be recorded for quality assurance purposes."
MAY be recorded, my ass.

Years of genuine care and interest in the customers—yes, even the idiots; they really couldn't help it—went out the window as the women were forced to spew robotic responses creating a frustrating loop-the-loop for customers:

CUST: I don't know how to program my new remote.
REP: I apologize for that inconvenience. You can find assistance in the instruction manual. I will send you a link for that document. May I help you with anything else?

CUST: I thought my blender had a three-month warranty instead of 30 days.
REP: I apologize for that inconvenience. You can find that information in our terms and conditions. I will send you a link for that document. May I help you with anything else?

CUST: The switch on my vacuum cleaner doesn't work right all the time.

REP: I apologize for that inconvenience. That is a manufacturer's issue. I will send you a link to their website. May I help you with anything else?

The "On My Last Day" book kept getting thicker, but now there was a special section directed at management, too:

- "How did someone that looks like you sleep your way to the top?"
- "Would you like to borrow my Chapstick? All that ass kissing must take a toll on your lips."
- "From now on, we're writing everything in cursive. Good luck figuring that out, Einstein."

It didn't take long for Kathy to decide it was time to call it quits. But, thanks to the good sense instilled in her generation, she wasn't going to just walk out without a plan. A catalog in the mail from the local junior college (yes, her generation went and got the mail from the mailbox on a regular basis—and even looked at it) provided the answer she needed.

She called the registrar's office and was delighted to find they still had human beings on the phone who were allowed to answer questions. She chose a course and gave her credit card number to the intelligent and helpful person on the other end of the line, who then repeated it back to make sure it was correct. *Maybe the good old days aren't completely gone after all.*

The eight-week course flew by, and Kathy passed with flying colors. To celebrate, she invited her closest friends from work out to dinner to explain her plan and see if they wanted in. They did, and when the bill came, she was a ninja, brandishing her credit card before anyone could even reach for a purse.

"My treat, little ladies," she said. "I've already decided to retire, but you're putting your own jobs on the line, so the least I can do is pay for our possible last supper."

On Kathy's last day, management was magnanimous and—despite it being *quite irregular*—allowed the colleagues from her shift to linger and have the cake they brought at 3:00 p.m. in the nearby breakroom. She was presented with a generous $50 Rainforest Peak gift certificate by her supervisor, who turned up her nose at the carb-laden cake, wished Kathy a tepid farewell, and beat a hasty retreat. The women took cake, filled their coffee cups, and turned their attention to the customer service department, where their cubicles were now filled with the Gen Z kids who cared even less about the customers than management did. They were happy to read from a script, and with just a little more energy and enthusiasm they might someday work their way up to being actual robots.

Though they wouldn't hear the callers, Kathy opened the break room door so they all could hear some of the responses. They were not disappointed.

REP: It sounds to me like you're trying to scam us out of another flat screen TV. This doesn't pass the sniff test.

REP: You must be a complete moron if you can't get a remote to work.

REP: Don't yell at me. I wasn't the idiot who bought from this stupid company.

REP: Go ahead and call my manager. He's an even bigger dick than you. You'll get along great.

REP: I don't know what you look like, lady, but I bet no amount of make up in the world is going to help.

On and on it went, straight from the pages of the "On My Last Day" playbook.

Some of the callers apparently made good on their threats to contact management, and before long the women were treated to Act Two of the delightful farce unfolding before them. Frantic managers flooded the room, shouting at the call center workers to stop talking, hang up, and log off.

"What in the actual fuck is going on?" one manager bellowed. "Why are you talking to customers like this?"

An unconcerned-looking twenty-something decided to answer for the group.

"We were, like, just reading the script like you told us to," she said, looking pained at her boss's ridiculous question. "I mean, like, I thought we would like get canned or something if we said anything that like wasn't in the script. Right?"

"Get up," he barked. The girl shrugged and did as she was told.

He sat at the screen and went to the program that generated the scripted response based on the audio from the customer. He clicked on the headset and, as if a customer, said, "When will my package arrive?" The scripted response popped up on the screen immediately: "How the hell should I know you lazy ass. Look at your order and find out for yourself."

Kathy and her friends clinked coffee cups as they watched the manager bury his head in his hands. They all turned and went back to get seconds on cake.

As the women dug in, two managers passed the open door, speaking loudly enough for all to hear.

"It's going to take a few days to get to the bottom of this," one said. "We'll send the girls home and put a message on the website that the phones are out and that people will have to use the online chat for customer service."

"Thank God that's totally automated," the other replied. "No idiot twenty-year-olds to tell customers to go screw themselves."

As their voices drifted off, Kathy set down her plate and took out her phone. As the women looked on, she went to the Rainforest Peak app and selected "Chat."

"If I order a dozen pairs of socks," she typed, "will I get 12 or 24?" She hit "Enter."

The response was instantaneous.

CHAT: Are you FUCKING kidding me?

~ The Prompt ~

Category:
Short Story

Genre:
Comedy

Object:
Credit card

Character:
A left-handed person

A Tale of a Fateful Trip

"Welcome to Waikiki, our next-to-last stop on your tour!"

The perky blonde smiled at the five travelers, winners of a promotion to send them on a Classic Television Super Fans Adventure Tour.

The group had worked its way across the continental United States, experiencing a recreation of Lucy and Ethel's candy wrapping fiasco, a failed dinner party in Mary Richards' apartment, and a night in a stately mansion in Beverly Hills, including a dip its famous ce-ment pond.

They were assembled in the lobby of Three Hour Tour, a popular tourist attraction that offered the full *Gilligan's Island* fan experience, sans storm and boat crash. The Skipper (an actual boat captain) and Gilligan (an actor) transported passengers to a small island where they stayed in replica huts for the weekend, replete with luxury glamping accommodations never seen onscreen.

"If you'll follow me," Perky Blonde continued, "we'll go into costuming, where you can decide on your roles and get ready to sail."

Thirty minutes later, their luggage stowed, Ginger, Mary Ann, the Professor, and Mr. and Mrs. Howell boarded the S.S. Minnow 2.0. They were enjoying champagne and hors d'oeuvres when a very authentic Skipper asked for their attention.

"Welcome aboard. My little buddy and I assure you this voyage will be much smoother sailing than that famous one everyone seems to know about."

"Well, I certainly hope so," said Mr. Howell, in a perfectly executed Larchmont lockjaw accent.

Passengers laughed; the Skipper continued.

"Before we get underway, I want to go over some safety items," he said. "Gilligan, please bring up a life vest to demonstrate."

A gangly, elastic-limbed young man, donning a red shirt and white bucket hat, tripped his way up to the Skipper, dropping the life vest three times en route. His demonstration of the proper use of the life vest somehow included attaching himself to both the Skipper and the railing, much to the delight of the passengers.

An authentic *Gilligan's Island* experience was underway.

As the captain manned the helm, the passengers fully embraced their roles.

Ginger, an IT manager, relished the attention she was getting in her backless, sequined evening gown from Mr. Howell, a financial advisor much younger than his character.

Mrs. Howell, a sixty-eight-year-old retired librarian, was asking Mary Ann, a college student bedecked in a gingham dress and full apron, how she knew about shows from forty years before she was born.

"My Grandma and I would watch the rerun channel. If she hadn't died last year, she'd be here instead of me. *She* was a super fan. I entered the contest for her."

As the other passengers were enjoying their cosplay, the Professor, carrying a briefcase, made his way toward the railing behind the helm.

"Hey everyone. That includes you, Skipper. I'd like to do an experiment."

"Wouldn't it be better to wait until we get to the island?" the Skipper said. "We'll be there in about an hour."

The Professor opened the briefcase and took out a revolver. Mary Ann screamed and began crying. Ginger instinctively put her arms around her and whispered not to worry.

"No, I think now's a better time," he said, jabbing the gun in his back. "Cut the engine and unplug the radio."

The Skipper complied and was ordered down to the deck with the others.

"Here's how it's going to go," the Professor said. "Everyone stays calm and nobody gets hurt. Hey, *little buddy*, grab that bucket by the railing. I want everyone's cell phone and smart watch in the bucket."

Gilligan did as he was told, as did the passengers.

"Now dump them overboard." Gilligan did.

"Okay. Everyone sit down and stay where I can see you. Not you, Skipper. You come up here. We're going to take a little detour."

The Professor had the captain sit down behind the wheel.

"We're going to adjust course due east from here," he said. "There's an uninhabited island you're taking us to."

He reached into the briefcase and handed over a paper with coordinates, careful not to show or spill any of the million dollars in stolen jewels he was hoarding inside.

"Start the engine and follow that course. And I don't want to see your hand anywhere near the radio."

"Why are you doing this?" Mr. Howell asked, now back to his normal speech.

"I have some business to take care of, and a boat is just what I need," he said. "Meanwhile, you all are going to get a truly authentic *Gilligan's Island* experience. Isn't that great?"

"This isn't a TV show," Mary Ann said. "We can't survive there."

"If you don't check in, they'll come looking. You'll be fine. C'mon, Skipper. Let's get moving."

Forty-five minutes later the group was forced to climb down the side ladder and began the difficult trek to shore. The Professor sped off in the boat; the wake knocking some of them to their knees.

Mary Ann was crying again, and Ginger told her not to worry.

"Don't worry? We just were almost killed, and now we're stranded here for God knows how long!"

Ginger smiled. "Check your apron pocket," she said. Mary Ann reached into the deep pocket and pulled out a smart watch.

"But how… when?"

"As soon as he pulled out the gun, I knew he was going to take our electronics," Ginger explained. "Remember when I came over to comfort you? I slipped it in then."

"That's genius," the Skipper said. "They'll find us, but that boat is going to be another story."

"Don't worry," Ginger said. "He thought of the phones and watches, but I doubt he'll remember the luggage in the hold. I never travel without an AirTag in my bag. They'll trace him right away."

Ginger made the emergency call on her watch as the others sat down in the sand.

"Holy shit," said Mr. Howell. "And here I thought they were saving the big adventure for next week in Korea at the 4077th."

~ The Prompt ~

Category: Flash Fiction

Genre: Shipwrecked

Character: Hoarder

Object: Life Vest

Beach Blanket Butchery

When a creep turns into a monster, even a pacifist can remain an innocent bystander for only so long.

I watch the sun glide over the horizon, turning the surface of the lake into a mirrored light show. This cosmic alarm clock wakes the birds, who began their morning chorus right on time.

But that bloated, bloody bastard on the beach will never wake up again.

His body is laying across the berm crest—that's the imaginary line that separates the foreshore and backshore. His pants still show the stain where he peed himself during the attack, but the rest of him is dry from the waist down. His top half is a different story.

The pool of blood has been washed away, but there's still some trickling from one of the gaping holes in his neck—probably where I hit the big vein. The rest of the holes, along with his mouth, ears, and nose, are being filled with sand, pebbles, and—I hope—tons of fish shit, thanks to those never-ending waves. Oh, look! A seagull just plucked out one of his eyeballs. Bon Appetit!

I never planned to kill him. Anybody that knows me knows I'm not the violent type. I keep to myself. Live and let live, that's my motto. Even with a scumbag like him. Yeah, I knew all about him and the horrible things he's done. I *saw* the horrible things he's done.

I live in a small place that overlooks the beach. I can see everything. This guy runs—well, I guess *ran*—a rental place on the beach for tourists. You know, umbrellas, swim fins, beach chairs. Been doing it as long as I've been here.

I've been watching *him* all that time, too. He used to be just a creep. Bullying little kids, leering at teenage girls, helping himself to people's stuff when they're in the water. Probably shortchanged people, too. Plays it nice for the rich tourists, but a shitty little jerk to everybody else.

This summer, it all changed. Something must have happened to make him snap. I don't get into town much—like I said, I keep to myself out here—but somebody insulted his mama or his manhood, or maybe his mama insulted his manhood. I don't know. But yeah, he snapped.

It was a couple weeks after the beach opened. Just after sundown when the beach is closed, I see him and a young girl go back to the rental hut. They leave the door open, and I can see her down on her knees in front of the guy. This goes on for a few minutes, then they both come out. As she turns her back to leave, he whacks her on the head with something heavy and knocks her out. He leans over, takes her head in his hands, and snaps her neck. I've seen that done to birds when they're injured to put them out of their misery. Made me want to puke. Then he drags her body into the sand where the waves are coming in and leaves her. He walks around the beach and gets rid of the drag marks, closes up shop and leaves.

And here's the kicker. The next morning, he's the first guy on the beach, just after sun-up. He calls the police. They must have believed his story because he never got arrested.

About a month later, I see him talking to this young man—not much more than a kid. The guy is showing him a snorkel—probably explaining how it works. All the while the guy is looking around, making sure nobody is noticing. Nobody is… except me. They talk for a while, shake hands, and the kid leaves. So, I wait. I know something's up.

Sure enough, after the beach closes, the kid comes back. The guy gets out the snorkel and helps the kid put it on. They go into the water for the lesson. The guy pushes the kid under the water until the air hose is underwater too and holds him there. The kid struggles a while, then stops moving. Once he's sure the kid's dead he lets him go.

He goes back to the hut and jimmies the lock on the door to make it look like the kid broke in after hours to help himself. When the police come in the morning, he gets off scot-free again.

Now, you probably wonder why I didn't go to the police.

Well, like I said before, live and let live. Besides, what could I say to the police? They wouldn't pay any attention to me. So yeah, I didn't do anything.

Until he came after my family.

Yesterday at closing time, just before he locks up, I see he has a new toy. An air rifle he's loading with lead shot. I know all about these rifles. They've killed a lot of us, so I'm paying close attention. He turns and looks straight at me and my babies.

"I'm sick and tired of you goddamn crows shitting on my beach," he screams, aiming the gun right at my nest. He fires and misses. That's the only starting gun I needed.

I swoop down. Without thinking he runs toward the water, dropping the gun and tripping over it, landing face up. I dig my claws into his chest and don't hesitate—puncturing his neck like a black-feathered jackhammer. I don't stop until I hit the gusher.

Now, I want everyone to understand that in normal, unprovoked circumstances, we crows are a peaceful bunch. You don't bother us; we don't bother you. But, as our bovine friends like to say, "you mess with the bull, you get the horns." Remember, they don't call us a *murder* of crows for nothing.

Oh, look. The police have arrived. I'd better grab that other eyeball before they take the body away. You know, even with me returning to the scene of the crime, I don't think they'll suspect a thing.

~ The Prompt ~

Category:
Flash Fiction

Genre:
Horror

Object:
A snorkel

Location:
A crow's nest

All I Want for Christmas

"We nearly have reached it but still must make haste,
For truly there isn't a moment to waste!"

Is he talking to me or himself? Oliver couldn't tell, and it didn't matter as the pudgy, balding man in red plaid hustled the seventeen-year-old down the flattened candy cane walkway toward the towering glass doors.

Based on his journey so far, Oliver wouldn't have blinked an eye if there was a dragon at the entrance, demanding a mystical password. Instead, as if on the threshold of any supermarket, the doors automatically opened as the pair approached.

This was *not* the Hy-Vee.

Oliver stood in the doorway, mouth agape, unable to move. Sven, a thousand year-plus veteran of S.W.E.E.T. (Santa's Workshop Elf Enrollment Team), was accustomed to this reaction. He guided Oliver into the explosion of color, sounds, and activity. It was Oz, and Wonderland, and the Chocolate Factory, and every glorious pop-up book Oliver's mother had ever read him all rolled into one explosively delightful package.

Sven smiled as Oliver spun in a slow circle and drank it all in—a ballerina gazing in awe upon the heretofore hidden magnificence of the world when the jewelry box is opened for the first time.

Sven drew his pocket watch and checked it against the countdown clock on the far wall. T-minus 6:03 to lift-off. He had no choice but to interrupt the reverie.

"My goodness, you've come on our busiest of days!
I've hardly a moment to show you our ways.
But show you I must, for there's work to be done
ere St. Nicholas chases the world's setting sun!"

Sven led Oliver past thousands of elves at work: attaching wheels to shiny tricycles; placing plastic stethoscopes into pink doctor's bags; combing long, flowing doll hair; gluing eyes on stuffed animals; putting tiny, multi-colored interlocking bricks into plastic bags for the first—and last—time they will all be together.

They rounded a corner into a dead end, facing a mirrored door labeled TSA: Toy Sleigh Access. Sven turned to Oliver and gestured to the door.

"Alas, I now must leave you; your assignment lies within.
But guiding you thus far, for me, a pleasure it has been.
I wish you every happiness from deep within my heart.
And as you've joined our family, you now will look the part."

Sven made a grand, sweeping gesture in front of Oliver, producing a billowing puff of red smoke. When it cleared, Sven was gone, and Oliver turned to the door. His Hawkeyes t-shirt, jeans, and trainers were gone, replaced by a green tunic, red and green striped tights, and pointy-toed jester shoes. Peeking out from underneath his pom-pom festooned elf hat were equally pointy ears.

Toto, I don't think we're in Iowa anymore.

Oliver opened the door and found himself in what seemed to be a shipping room. There was an empty chair next to an elf that looked to be about his age.

“Hey, man, welcome,” he said, extending his hand. “I’m Ming Jié, but just call me Ming. You just get here?”

“Oliver,” he said, shaking hands. “Yeah, a little while ago, though I’m still not sure I’m not dreaming all this.”

“We all feel that way at first. But man, you picked a heckuva first day! Though none of us really picked, right?”

Before Oliver could ask him to explain further, a loud bell rang.

“Showtime, man,” Ming said. “You just watch for a while and you’ll catch on real quick, I know it.”

At first, Oliver wasn’t so sure about that. A loudspeaker was spewing a constant stream of addresses, names, ages, and, for some reason, saying “wrapped” or “unwrapped.” Then Ming would type something into the computer, a green light would come on, and gifts would appear on a conveyer belt—some wrapped, some not—which would then get hurled by other elves up into some kind of tunnel and disappear.

A few hours later, when Santa and the gang were flying over the Pacific toward Asia, Ming explained.

“Elves running reconnaissance on the sleigh transmit their location, which kids are next, and if the gifts need to be wrapped. I verify in the computer, distribution spits them out and they go up through the portal to Santa’s bag.”

The night and time zones passed quickly, and before Oliver knew it, Santa was nearing Des Moines. “South Rosebud Avenue,” the loudspeaker announced. “Joseph, six, 4550, wrapped; Oliver ten and Mary four, 4552, unwrapped; Jenny, eight, 4554, unwrapped…”

Ming was typing away and gifts were flying until the computer gave a loud error sound, and the conveyor belt light flashed red.

“Des Moines, we have a problem,” Ming said into his headset. “Hold on while I check.”

He searched and then got back on the headset.

“Skip Jenny at 4554. Last minute arrival today; computer was not updated in time.”

"Roger that. Continuing with South Rosebud Avenue. Lilly, three, 4556, wrapped…"

"That happens sometimes," Ming said. Oliver was ashen. "You okay, man?"

"That's my address. Jenny is my sister. I remember now. What did you mean, arrived today? What's going on?"

Ming called out, "Julia, please take over."

He stood and motioned for Oliver to come with him. "I have something to show you."

They walked back through the workshop, most of the elves now sitting with their feet up, and continued to a glassed-in area marked, "Playroom." Ming led Oliver to the glass.

"These are the two-to-eight-year-olds," he said. "They arrive too young to build toys, and since no one here ever gets any older, Petrov came up with the playroom. They couldn't have a happier eternity."

"So, we're dead?" Oliver asked.

"Well, you died, this morning, on your way to your grandmother's house. But I wouldn't call you dead. You've just moved on to your next life. Pretty cool, huh?"

Oliver scanned the playroom and saw Jenny, giggling with delight at a kitchen set with two other kids.

"Yeah. Pretty cool."

~ The Prompt ~

Category: Flash Fiction

Genre: Fantasy

Location: A Shared Workspace

Object: Wrapping Paper

Secrets and Surprises at the Fox River Lodge

The hard, skinny edge of the tub is digging into my tailbone, but I can't move. Maybe if I sit quietly and stare at the tiny rectangle long enough, the word "NOT" will magically appear in front of the word that just materialized. C'mon. You can do it. Appear, goddammit!

I rub my eyes; a final, ridiculous attempt to see something different. But the word is still there:

PREGNANT

Jeez, in the old days, at least you got a few more seconds of hope while you dug the box out of the trash to see what two lines meant. Now they just slap you right across the face with it.

I bury the test stick at the bottom of the trash can with the packaging.

How are we going to manage with a baby? We barely scrape by, and we're on top of each other here. I want a baby with Matt, but not now. We need to get back on our feet first, be in a proper home. What in God's name is he going to say?

And Keira? She already hates me, the wicked stepmother who ruined her life. She'll blame me, think I did it on purpose. All part of my calculated plan to…

I jump as pounding rattles the flimsy door.

"Did you fall in, Jenn? Are you almost done or should I walk down to the gas station?"

I open the door.

"Sorry. All yours."

She steps aside to let me exit. It's not courtesy, but disdain. She is loath to even look at me; physical contact—even an inadvertent brush while passing—is out of the question.

She slams the door, and I marvel at the memory of the comparatively delightful girl I met four years ago.

She was friendly, if a little wary. After all, it had been just her and Matt for all eleven years of her life, and I was an interloper.

But one of the good things about a prepubescent girl is that, just like her breasts, the chip on her shoulder hadn't come in yet either, which made my entrée into their life a bit easier. Plus, most kids that age still think the simpler things in life are fun: the zoo, ice cream, bowling.

Matt and I implemented a methodically planned schedule of special events to erode her armor, but ultimately the ace up my sleeve did the trick.

"You're a hairdresser?" Keira had squealed. "Oh my God! Do you do nails and makeup too? Can you pierce my ears? That's so cool!"

"Slow down, honey," Matt said. "Remember you're only eleven."

Keira rolled her eyes. I gave her a "don't worry" look and proceeded to set her father straight.

"Actually, she's almost twelve, Matt, and that's a very important age for a young lady. We don't have to go crazy, but I think maybe a new style and some subtle highlights would be just the thing for the first day of seventh grade."

She nearly tackled me with a bear hug, while Matt beamed and gave me a thumbs up sign. I was in.

There are three seats that magically motivate people to open up: a bar stool, the passenger seat of a car, and a salon chair. As I wrapped strands of Keira's hair in foil, she provided an animated account of her life. Where they'd lived, good and horrible teachers, her best friend, favorite foods. She even confided the name of the tall, blond boy who was her crush.

"Don't you dare say a word to Dad!" she said.

"Pinky swear," I promised.

In turn, I gave her the scoop on how her dad and I met.

"He came in late on a Friday afternoon with no appointment, and I was free. He sat down in the same chair you're in now, and we started talking. It was my night to close the shop, so before you knew it, we were all alone. He told me about his photography business and about his smart, beautiful daughter—all the important stuff. Next thing you know, he was sweeping up hair so I could lock the door and we could go to dinner. I think he left the salon with only half a haircut!"

Keira giggled at the story and then burst into even bigger gales of laughter as she caught sight of her bobbing, silver head in the mirror.

It wasn't until a few months later, after Matt and I were engaged, that she finally talked about her mother.

"I never knew my mom," she said. "When I was little and asked why I didn't have a mom like other kids, he'd just say, 'some families are just a dad and a daughter, like us.' But I kept asking, so when I was ten, Dad said I was old enough to know the truth. Mom got sick when I was just a baby, with cancer. They tried to make her well, but it didn't work. Dad said he was holding me and that the last thing she said before she died was my name."

Keira turned her head, embarrassed that I might see her tears. What a wonderful man Matt was, comforting his daughter by fabricating a tender tale to memorialize her monster of a mother.

We'd been dating a few weeks when Matt told me the truth. It was shortly after their third anniversary. They had just built a new house when she found out she was pregnant. Matt was overjoyed, but his wife was horrified. What made him think she'd ever wanted kids? She had her career to think about, her future. He could beg all he wanted, but she was going to get an abortion.

He finally used the only weapon in his arsenal—money. He had a trust fund that had come from his grandparents that would have made them set for life. He realized too late it was the only reason she'd married him.

Matt made her a proposition. If she had the baby and signed away her parental rights, he would give her everything; no strings attached. She could start a new life without him. The wife agreed.

Keira was born, the paperwork was signed, and she and Matt rented the basement apartment of a friend of his parents. He turned a storage room into a darkroom and started his own photography business, specializing in weddings and other remote events. He never got rich, but he always had enough to get by. It was cozy, but they made room for one more when we got married two years ago.

In retrospect, it may not have been the best timing to thrust such a big change on a new teenager, who no longer could be enticed by miniature golf and a haircut. Keira remained mostly civil to me, but clearly no longer thought of me as her cool new girlfriend. Yet we managed.

Until spring of 2020.

COVID was hard on everyone, but it decimated us. My salon was shuttered, and every wedding, quinceañera, bar mitzvah, and corporate event on Matt's calendar was cancelled. We went from a simple, but comfortable existence to flat broke faster than you could say hydroxychloroquine.

We were grateful we had a place to live with a compassionate landlord who took mercy on our situation. Unemployment benefits allowed us to keep food on the table, and despite all of us being home all day, every day, we coped.

Then, just as things were starting to open back up, and we dared to be cautiously optimistic, the bottom of the bottom fell out.

Our landlord, the only tenuous connection we had to survival, contracted COVID and died. His children, themselves struggling financially, had no choice but to sell the house. We had thirty days to find a place to live.

Which is what brought us to the Fox River Lodge, a dilapidated motel about an hour west of the city. I used to pass this place on my way to work every morning. Raggedy kids stood at the edge of the parking lot with their parents, waiting for the school bus under the teetering sign that offered daily, weekly, and monthly rates. I couldn't imagine the rock bottom you'd have to hit to bring your family to a place like this. I felt so sorry for all of them.

Well, now it's us, and Keira is one of those kids. In one of the few silver linings of COVID, she is spared the indignity of the school bus thanks to remote learning.

We were also lucky that there was what they boldly called a "suite" available when we checked in: besides the main room and kitchenette, there was a separate bedroom with a door. We've been here five months and, so far, no bed bugs or roaches. A nominal blessing I force myself to count daily.

I go into the bedroom, pull the thin curtains back and look out on the so-called recreation area. A tattered net hangs from a rusty basketball hoop on a patch of concrete. Two picnic tables are nearby on the islands of brown grass amidst the dirt.

Taylor, the forty-something single mom two doors down, sits at one of the tables and folds laundry as her five- and six-year-old sons push dollar store trucks through the dirt. She lights a cigarette and watches them. The younger boy runs to her, presenting some treasure unearthed from the hard ground, and she reacts as if it's the archeological find of the century. Against all odds, the small family appears happy.

I wish I could say the same for Keira. If our mostly peaceful coexistence was a house of cards, the move here was the table bump that sent it all crashing down. Overnight, Keira became a powder keg, and it took nothing to light the fuse. She vacillated between angry rants and cold-blooded silence. She hated this place; she hated her father. She hated me; she hated life.

At first, Matt and I tried to appease her. But months of her venom, on top of our own lives crumbling before our eyes, eventually wore us down. Now, we all just try to keep our distance and tiptoe on the eggshells that cover every inch of the floor.

I sit down on the double bed and look around. If we take out the nightstands and move the bed against the wall, we might be able to squeeze in a crib. Oh my God. A baby. What next?

Keira appears in the doorway.

"Where's Dad? When's he getting home? What's for dinner?"

Holy shit. It speaks! And three sentences. My diary is going to be full tonight.

"He and Kenny got a job installing gutters at a house in Elburn. He thought they'd be done by five and he's going to bring something home. Anything sound good to you?"

"Whatever," she says, and trudges back to the couch.

My phone rings. Kenny.

"Hi Kenny. What's—"

He cuts me off.

"There's been an accident, Jenn. Matt was pulling off the old gutter and there was a wasp nest underneath. He was stung dozens of times and fell off the ladder. They're taking him to Mercy in Aurora. You need to get there right away. It's bad Jenn. Really bad. I'm on my way there now…are you there, Jenn? Do you understand?"

I manage to croak "okay" and Kenny disconnects. I know I need to get to the hospital, but I'm paralyzed. Keira is back in the doorway.

"What's wrong?"

For the first time in weeks, her face shows an emotion besides anger. I literally shake my head to clear it and stand up.

"Your dad's been hurt on the job," I say. "Grab your purse. We need to go to the hospital."

We make the thirty-minute drive in terrified silence. I know her mind is spinning out of control the same as mine. I try to make the flood of questions stop, but they are relentless.

Why did Kenny tell me it was really bad? How bad? Will Matt be okay? Is he allergic to wasps? Is that what's bad, or was it the fall? Will I be able to take care of him and support us? What if Matt dies?

The car screeches into the parking lot and we race for the emergency room. After donning masks and passing our temperature tests, we find Kenny in the waiting room. He pulls us both close.

"Is Dad okay?" Keira begs.

"The doctor hasn't been out."

"Please tell us what happened."

"Like I said, he somehow woke up this wasp nest that was under the old gutters. I've never seen anything like it. It was like something from an Alfred Hitchcock movie. They just swarmed his head. He was trying to bat them away and hold on at the same time, and then he fell off the ladder from two stories up."

Keira begins sobbing. I put my arm around her, and she lets it stay.

"I called 911. I didn't want to move him because of the fall. Thank God the squad got there fast, because his whole face was swelling up. I don't think he could breathe. One of the paramedics pulled out an EpiPen and gave him a shot. Then they put him on a backboard, told me where they were taking him, and raced off. Then I called you. I don't know if he was breathing or not when they left."

It was unfathomable. We stand here, not knowing if Matt is dead or alive. We sit down, but Kenny immediately gets up to pace.

"I can't just sit," he says. "I'm going to get us all something to drink."

Keira and I sit in silence for a few more minutes, her sobs having turned to occasional, sniffly hiccups.

"I know my mom's not dead."

The pregnancy test had slapped me in the face. This was a Muhammad Ali uppercut.

I start to answer, but she continues.

"When we had to move, I was helping Dad pack his work stuff. One day when he wasn't there, I was putting things from his file cabinet into boxes, and way at the back was an envelope that said divorce settlement. I was nosy and opened it."

Keira digs into the depths of her enormous purse and pulls out papers.

"So, I know that my mother isn't dead." She hangs her head. "And I know she doesn't want me."

She begins crying again and buries her face against me.

"I'm so sorry, Jenn. I know I've been a bitch to you and Dad. First COVID, and then we had no money, and then we had to move to that shitty place, and on top of everything I find out THIS! And now dad might die and then what am I gonna do if my own mother doesn't want me?"

I hold on tight as sobs wrack her body. When they subside, I take her by the shoulders and look her straight in the eye.

"First of all, you dad isn't going to die. He's going to be okay. He has to because...we're going to have a baby."

"What?"

"Yes. Believe me, I'm as shocked as you are. But that's why I know he's going to be okay."

I feel some tension go out of her and I see a slight smile start to form.

"And second, you are absolutely wrong about your mother not wanting you."

"But the papers—"

"Fuck those papers. Your mother wants you more than anything else in the world. Do you want to know how I know?"

She nods.

"Because *I'm* your mother. Like it or not, *I'm* your mother and you're stuck with me, shitty motel and all. *I'm* your mother, and I wouldn't have it any other way. *I'm* your mother, and I will always want you. You got that?"

She nods again and hugs me tight. I see a doctor coming toward us and realize I'm no longer afraid of what he's going to say. Somehow, I know everything is going to be all right.

~ The Prompt ~

Category:
Short Story

Character:
A step-parent

Location:
A run-down motel

Must include:
A wasp nest

Scene Stealer

Sharpshooters played a perilous game of Ring Around the Rosie as Mills clutched the vial in his outstretched hand. Was it the deadly contagion or a decoy? Those watching were transfixed.

Suddenly, a blue flash appeared from nowhere and streaked toward Mills. He dropped the vial.

The SWAT Team converged as the superhero intercepted the falling object just in time. Everyone cheered.

"I'm back," a beautiful blonde whispered in Jeff's ear. He relinquished the seat.

As the announcer boomed, "The Oscar for achievement in special effects goes to. . ." Jeff exited with the blonde's diamond bracelet in his pocket.

~ The Prompt ~

Category: Nanofiction

Genre: Action/Adventure

Action: Pickpocketing

Word: Achieve

Play Dough, Story Time, and the Scales of Justice

They say everything you need to know you learn in kindergarten. Including justice.

Colton Griffin shuffled as he was led into the courtroom. His manacled hands and feet clanked an unwavering dirge while his orange jumpsuit and bleached hair contrasted sharply with the black backdrop of the dimly lit, windowless room.

The nineteen-year-old sat at the defendant's table, oblivious to the bursting gallery of spectators. With a force and accuracy major league pitchers would envy, a woman in the front row launched a glob of spit onto Griffin's cheek. As it stuck, the crowd laughed and officials turned a blind eye. There were no Colton Griffin fans in the courtroom.

"All rise! Court is now in session. The Honorable Helgen Petros presiding."

The public defender jostled Griffin to his feet as the judge took the bench.

"Be seated," Petros said. He turned to the plaintiff's table. "You have the floor, Madam Prosecutor."

"Thank you, your honor. We are here today to pronounce sentence on convicted school shooter Colton Griffin."

Hearing his name, Griffin turned a confused face to the prosecutor. He still didn't understand how he got there or what was happening.

"He killed my granddaughter!" a woman screamed from the back of the gallery. "She was just in kindergarten. He shot her in the face while she was playing dress-up. He's a monster. No punishment is enough."

The woman broke down and others began shouting. The judge banged his gavel.

"Order, please. I know this is an emotional day, but we have already heard your individual statements and must follow proper procedure to pass sentence. Please continue, Madam Prosecutor."

"If it please the court, before we receive the jury's verdict, I would like to briefly recount the tragic events of October 18, 2023, that took place at Prairie Springs Elementary School."

Griffin looked to his right, past the plaintiff's table. *Where's the jury? All I see is a mirror.*

"On that Wednesday morning, Colton Griffin used a high-powered automatic weapon to shoot through the emergency exit door of a kindergarten classroom. He then proceeded—deliberately and with malice aforethought—to discharge his weapon in the direction of the two teachers and ten students in the room."

The prosecutor's words came to life in holographic imagery at the front of the courtroom, and the heretofore quiet sobbing from the gallery transformed into heart-wrenching wails.

Griffin scanned the room. *How are they doing that? Where's the projector?*

"As you can see, both teachers instinctively threw themselves in front of the students to shield them, and each was killed instantly."

Someone in the gallery screamed in anguish as one teacher was scalped by the spray of bullets, her remaining blonde hair now turning red as it was saturated with her own blood. The other teacher's mortal wounds were mercifully out of the picture.

Where'd they get this video? I didn't see any cameras.

"Once Griffin had taken care of the teachers, he made sure he hadn't missed any of the students, as some had been in play areas in other parts of the classroom. He didn't shoot until each was looking him in the eye."

On screen, Griffin sprayed the group of five-year-olds with the nonchalance of someone watering flowers. A pigtailed girl in a polka dot dress grabbed her stomach and fell forward onto her already-dead playmate. After kicking another child with his blood-stained shoe to make sure the kid was dead, Griffin methodically picked off the children in the fringes of the room one-by-one. His final monstrous act was to point and laugh at a little red-haired boy who had wet his pants before aiming the machine gun between his eyes.

"And then, as the SWAT team approached the building, Colton Griffin confirmed his cowardice by taking his own life."

Spectators cheered as they watched Griffin remove a handgun from his belt, put it to his ear, and pull the trigger. The hologram dissolved.

What the hell? Griffin reached up and felt the gaping hole in the non-spit-covered side of his head.

"I'm dead?" he shouted.

"Well, of course, Mr. Griffin," Judge Petros answered. "Didn't you see the pearly gates outside?"

"So, I'm in…"

"You're getting ahead of yourself, Mr. Griffin. What happens next is up to the jury."

The judge turned toward the mirror, which vanished, revealing the jury box. Each of the twelve seats were filled with body bags; two large and ten small.

"Ladies and gentlemen of the jury," the judge said. "You may divulge your identities to the defendant."

The body bags dissolved, revealing the kindergarten teachers and their ten students. The spectators—their pre-deceased loved ones who had welcomed them to their new eternal home—were now sobbing with joy at the sight of their once again whole and healthy bodies and spirits.

"Is the jury ready to pronounce sentence on Colton Griffin?"

The group had unanimously chosen the little red-haired boy as its foreman, and he stood to his full (and forever) height of forty-four inches.

"Yes, your honor," he said. "Colton Griffin was mean and a bully and then he killed all of us. Even though our teachers say it's never good to be mean back to bullies, we think he deserves punishment for what he did. So, we're sending him to a place where everyone he meets will call him names and treat him mean and make him feel bad about himself and be embarrassed. Maybe someday, if he learns to be nice, he can have a second chance, like we give people in kindergarten. But that's up to you, your honor."

"I will certainly give that some thought," the judge said. "For now, sentencing is approved, and the jury is dismissed."

As the guard led Griffin past the jury box, the little red-haired boy pointed and doubled over in laughter.

Griffin looked down. Without knowing it—and not for the last time—he had wet his pants.

~ The Prompt ~

Category:
Flash Fiction

Genre:
Horror

Location:
A Courthouse

Object:
A Body Bag

School's Out

Three in one day. Had it ever been done before? If a serial killer of his caliber and infamy had never done it, no one had.

It was a productive day already. He had swooped in like a stealth bomber and attacked two schools. Attempts to scatter and hide proved futile, and he departed the killing spree filled with the strange sensation of satisfaction coupled with a magnetic hunger for more.

An obsession with hunting down and viciously eliminating his victims defined his life. Decades ago, he had been satisfied with killing one person at a time. The savagery of his conquests dominated the media; his description on everyone's lips. Despite the notoriety, and a panic unlike any seen before or since, he was never captured and the hysteria and paranoia eventually faded.

At that time, he thought mass killings uncouth, the lazy enterprise of an amateur assassin. But age, along with an ever-increasing blood lust, convinced him to adopt the old adage: work smart, not hard. Where better to implement this streamlined strategy than in the vulnerable environment of a school?

The area was densely populated. Schools were everywhere, but with enough distance between to provide a nearly unlimited supply of potential victims. He was a pro and moved with a speed and elegance that allowed him to survey, attack, and escape without capture or retaliation from either inside or outside the school.

His internal radar never faltered, and he was always at the ready should an opportunity arise, as it had right now.

The school seemed to have materialized right before his eyes. Unlike the two he'd hit earlier, this one was small, its occupants clearly part of a unique and exclusive community. He looked into the school, where the eclectic grouping formed a colorful, flowery mural against a blue backdrop.

He deftly circled, watching for suspicious eyes, but saw none. This part of the process was critical. Once committed, he must be lightning fast and decisive. A moment's hesitation was all it took to drastically reduce the spoils of his game.

In a flash he was inside the school, heading first for the adults. The scared, slower children would be his shortly. Bedlam erupted.

Blood was everywhere, adding to the panic and confusion. Some escaped, but most were not so lucky, their faces frozen in a silent scream. Within minutes it was over, and he knew he didn't have the luxury of basking in the aftermath of his horrifying handiwork.

As he turned tail to leave, he sensed shadowy movement above him, followed by an agonizing, and fatal, pain in his back.

Above the water, a fisherman whooped with delight and began to pull in the line.

"I got him with the harpoon gun!" he squealed. "I got the shark!"

~ The Prompt ~

Category: Flash Fiction

First Word of the Story: Three

Setting: A School

Must include the adjectives:
Magnetic, Uncouth, Suspicious, Flowery

Jimmy the Geek

Assessing odds was Jimmy's superpower.
But what happens when the oddsmaker's luck runs out?

Jimmy was afraid. This was uncharted territory for him and, if there was one thing that made him feel secure, it was charts. Nonetheless, he knew it had to be done. He swiped right.

Allison set down the magazine. Every time she read it, a combination of grief and rage boiled inside her. How long would it be before she could take revenge? A ping on her phone shifted her attention. She opened the dating app, smiled, and responded.

Jimmy knew better than anyone the odds of success through a dating app were terrible. Actually, Jimmy knew the odds of *everything* better than anyone. As a kid, his nerdy interest in probability and statistics got the pudgy, bespectacled adolescent stuffed in lockers and stripped of his lunch money.

It didn't take him long, though, to figure out that bullies love something even more than torture: money. Capitalizing on their greed as well as their lust for crushing the proverbial little guy, he mentored the hoodlums-in-training until every boy's bathroom in the district was running a floating craps game.

Jimmy knew a good thing when he saw it and decided to become a professional oddsmaker. But after college, despite contact lenses and a Peleton-esque body, he just couldn't shake the nerd persona. After failed attempts to break into the tight-knit world of odds making in the gambling and political arenas, he faced the truth: Vegas wanted Jimmy the Greek, not Jimmy the Geek.

Luckily, there was one other arena that couldn't rake in their billions without expert knowledge of the odds: the insurance industry. Jimmy became an actuary.

His prodigious ability shot him up the corporate ladder at Consolidated Representors and Protectors, the largest insurance conglomerate in the tri-state area. Sure, he occasionally felt like he was back in that middle school bathroom, but being respected and doing what he loved helped him shake off that sense of déjà vu. He managed a team of ten, but kept his own skills sharp, as multi-million-dollar decisions lived or died by the stroke of his pen.

Nonetheless, being a rich genius can be a lonely existence, especially when risk statistics and actuarial tables are all you can muster for scintillating conversation. He knew this date with a beautiful redhead was a one-in-a-million chance for love. What he didn't know was that the odds were still out on whether he would live to enjoy it.

Allison signed up for online dating for a different reason. She had spent the last six months as her grandfather's caretaker, watching him die a painful, miserable death from his rare cancer. The disease had stripped her beloved Poppy of his physical and mental faculties, dignity, and life savings.

Because there was no money for paid nurses, Allison had taken a leave of absence from her job, given up her apartment, and moved in with Poppy. He had promised she could stay in the house after he was gone, but it would just be a matter of time before that belonged to the bank.

It wasn't supposed to be this way. Long before Poppy got sick, he and Allison had sat down with an agent and bought what was described as the best Medicare supplement around. If he paid his monthly premiums, he wouldn't have to worry about a thing.

"But what about if I get cancer?" Poppy asked, remembering the horror of losing his beloved wife years earlier.

"Not to worry," assured the agent. "It's all covered. Rest easy."

Not a word of it had been true.

Sure, when a routine scan discovered the very rare but treatable cancer, Poppy was able to see an oncologist and begin traditional chemotherapy. When there was no improvement, Allison sat with Poppy in the oncologist's office.

"I'm afraid chemo hasn't worked," the doctor said. Allison and Poppy looked at each other with despair.

"The only thing left to try is an experimental treatment..."

"That's great!" Allison interrupted. "When can Poppy start?"

"Well," the doctor continued, "before he can begin, we need to get the okay from the insurance company."

"That won't be a problem," Poppy said. "I was told I had nothing to worry about—even cancer."

"You'd better check with the insurance company just to be sure," the doctor said, with no hint of optimism in his voice.

A week later, the letter came, on official Consolidated Representors and Protectors letterhead, expressing sincere regret that the treatment couldn't be approved because of its "experimental nature and unproven results."

"What the hell do they think experimental means?" Allison screamed. "We're going to fight this, Poppy."

Whether from the wisdom of age (and decades fighting City Hall in vain) or exhaustion from treatment, Poppy told Allison he just wanted a peaceful end in the home he had shared with his wife. It came six weeks later.

That was three months ago, and Allison had been searching for a way to get back at the insurance company. *Goddamn snake oil salesman. There's a special place in hell for people who cheat the elderly. And I'm going to make sure he gets there.*

Her answer came in yesterday's mail.

"Forty Under Forty" was the name of the piece in the business magazine, profiling young leaders in their fields. And there he was, James Fleekner, Vice President of Actuarial Operations at Consolidated Representors and Protectors.

"An actuary is like a Vegas oddsmaker," Fleekner had explained in the article. "But instead of looking at the health of a horse, or the skill of a basketball player, we assess risk. We need to know the risks that will come from insuring a person so we can create plans and set premiums based on how likely it is we will have to pay out a claim."

He killed Poppy. And I have to kill him.

When the reporter asked about his being single, he joked about all his statistical charts not helping and confessed to giving online dating a try.

Allison went all in.

Jimmy couldn't believe what he was seeing in Allison's profile. Not only was she beautiful, but she also loved reading, mathematics, and logic puzzles, was a finance major in college, and "was a nerd in high school who learned how to make the most of it in the real world."

Allison and Jimmy became inseparable. She deftly probed him about his job and feigned enthusiasm for all the jibber jabber about risk, statistics, and probability.

Jimmy, flabbergasted that a woman was interested in both him *and* his work, did not hold back. He took her to former accident sites and pointed out high-risk areas and sloppy safety practices. He duly informed her about life expectancies, and the factors that determined same. The flowers he brought were often accompanied by interesting trade journal articles, or books full of little-known facts.

They never saw each other on Tuesday nights, when Allison attended her grief support group. While the grief she still felt for Poppy was genuine, her motive for attending the group was not.

One by one she connected with the younger men in the group, listening to their stories and relaying her own anger at the insurance company which she knew had caused her grandfather's early death. On week three, she hit paydirt.

Mike and Gary were brothers whose mother, Rose, had died at fifty-eight from ovarian cancer. She had been denied treatment by Consolidated Representors and Protectors because her most recent payment was late and her coverage canceled. When Rose called, they agreed to reinstate her policy after payment of the premium and a late fee, but her cancer was now a preexisting condition and would not be covered until a year after the new starting date. She was dead long before then.

A triumvirate was now out to get James Fleekner.

Allison didn't read the books Jimmy gave her, but she'd read enough true crime stories to know that this process couldn't be rushed. She diligently nurtured her growing relationship with Jimmy, gaining his unconditional trust.

Meanwhile, she, Mike, and Gary had long since ditched the grief support sessions. Instead, they met at Rose's house to lay out step-by-step scenarios that would leave Jimmy dead and their loved ones vindicated.

Jimmy knows about odds, but we're holding all the cards.

Late in October, after an Indian summer weekend spent strolling through the city with Jimmy, Allison showed up on Tuesday night and told the guys she had the perfect location and plan. And, in a beautiful irony, the person who had provided it all for them was Jimmy.

Allison told Jimmy she had some friends who wanted to meet him and invited them over for dinner. When the couple showed up at Rose's house that night, Mike and Gary were waiting with all the tools needed to get Jimmy bound and into the back of their panel van.

As Mike drove and Gary rode shotgun, Allison sat in the back with Jimmy.

"What is going on, Allison?" Jimmy pleaded. "Who are these two guys? Why did you let them do this to me?"

"They aren't doing it, Jimmy. We all are."

"I don't understand. Why?"

"You killed my grandfather," Allison replied, showing no emotion. "And you killed their mother, Rose."

"Damn right!" shouted Gary from the front.

"Shut up," said Mike. "Let her do this."

"I've never met your Poppy…"

"Don't call him that!" Allison screeched. "You aren't allowed to call him that!"

"But Allison, I didn't know your grandfather or their mother," Jimmy said. "What do you mean I killed them?"

"You and your precious risk factors, that's how," she spat. "Your goddamn insurance company found loopholes so they were denied treatment."

Allison closed her eyes and took a breath to calm herself. "And as you have told me—ad nauseum, I might add—the cornerstone of the insurance agency, the reason it can stay in business, is the genius actuary who assesses risk."

She looked him straight in the eye, her pupil's black as night. "That's you."

"We're here," Mike yelled, as the van slowed and pulled off the road.

He and Gary got out and opened the back of the van. Like Alison, they were dressed all in black and would be well-hidden from any onlookers on the cloudy, moonless night.

"Looks clear," said Gary.

Allison scooched along the floor of the van and out the back door. Mike and Gary reached in and dragged Jimmy out.

Jimmy turned and saw they were at the edge of a remote bridge on the outskirts of the city. The water slid silently by, far below them. There were no cars, houses, or people in sight.

"Remember what you told me when we came here last weekend?" Allison asked. "I usually tune out your stupid, useless drivel, but this fact proved to be important."

"What's happening, Allison?" Jimmy asked.

She ignored his question. "You told me that, even though we were outside the city, this was a significant place because it's the site of so many suicides."

She picked up a large rock and threw it over the side. It took several seconds before the splash broke the tense silence.

"So, I figured what better place for you to get yours," Allison continued. "That water looks pretty cold. It's not going to take long."

"Allison, don't do this," Jimmy begged. "I'll go to the president of the company Monday. We'll make it right."

"That's a lie," Gary said, tightening his grip on Jimmy's arm. "Besides, money isn't going to bring back our mom or her grandfather."

"I know that," Jimmy said, desperately trying to think of something else to say to stall them. "You won't get away with this," he added. "Is this worth going to jail for?"

"There won't be any jail," Allison said, smiling. "You've guaranteed that." She motioned to Mike and Gary. "Untie him, but keep a good hold on him."

She returned her gaze to Jimmy.

"You're just going to be another one of those statistics you love so much. When the authorities come to me, I'll tell them I broke up with you and, seeing how I was your first serious girlfriend, you just couldn't take it. They'll buy that in a New York minute." Allison smiled again. "Looks like you weren't such a genius about life expectancies after all. At least not your own.

"Goodbye, Jimmy. Enjoy that special place in hell reserved for insurance actuaries."

As Mike and Gary fought to drag a struggling Jimmy to the siderail on the bridge, the area was suddenly awash in light—first bright white, quickly followed by flashing blue and red.

"Stop where you are," an amplified voice boomed.

Everyone froze in place, and two uniformed police officers walked through the shining light onto the scene.

"What's going on here?" one officer asked. "Why are you holding that man?"

Mike and Gary let go of Jimmy.

"Were they holding you against your will, sir?" the other officer asked.

Jimmy looked to Allison, hoping for a glimmer of remorse. Her eyes were cold.

"Yes, officer," he replied." They—all three of them—abducted me and were going to throw me in the river, hoping it would look like a suicide."

A second squad car arrived as the officers moved to handcuff Mike and Gary.

Jimmy walked over to Allison.

"So much for your damn probability," she said. "Sometimes it just comes down to bad luck."

"I beg to differ," Jimmy replied. "You should have known this would turn out this way."

"How so?" Allison asked.

"If you'd listened to everything I said last weekend, you would have also heard that because this is a prime location for suicides, it's under higher-than-average police patrol. I knew if I stalled long enough, someone would show up in time."

Another officer approached and placed handcuffs on Allison. As he began to lead her away, she turned to Jimmy and smiled. "How about we give it another try once I'm out of jail?" she asked.

He gave her a textbook poker face.

"I wouldn't bet on it."

~ The Prompt ~

Category:
Short story

Genre:
Suspense

Action:
A rip-off

Character:
An oddsmaker

Something Old, Something New, Something Manipulated, Something True

Everyone sitting in the church is smiling and playing nice.
But inside all the players' heads, they're throwing shade, not rice.

A year or two of planning has gone into this big day.
The mothers of the bride and groom have had a lot to say.
It's all been very cordial; neither one would be unkind.
Let's listen to their thoughts and hear what's really on their mind:

Mother of the Bride
My Katie beams with happiness; at peace and unconcerned.
To think had I not intervened, this would have crashed
 and burned.

That Adam's such a stubborn goat who has to have his way.
I guess his dad forgot to tell him grooms don't have a say.
Apparently, his mother also missed the scuttlebutt:
that she's supposed to dress in beige and keep her big mouth shut.

I first began with Katie, sharing tricks to deal with men.
"And if you play your cards right, he won't interfere again."
With Adam it was easy; what a sucker to be led.
Convincing him that Katie's plans were really his instead.

And then I took it one more step to make him feel quite glad.
I told him we were thrilled he'd be the son we never had.

I'll be the unsung hero; just relieved it all worked out.
And lauding me with praise is not what this day's all about.

I only wanted Katie on display for all to see.
Besides, I do not like it when the spotlight is on me.

Mother of the Groom

My Adam beams with happiness; at peace and unconcerned.
To think had I not intervened, this would have crashed
 and burned.

That Katie has a stubborn streak; three guesses at its source.
Her mother's constant meddling could have thrown this
 all off course.

That nut job made an awful scene; I had to acquiesce.
And all because my gown's dark green was too close to her dress.

She clearly thinks the groom's just there to do as he is told.
The last piece of the puzzle to be forced into their mold.

I had a talk with Adam; offered hints both small and large
So Katie and her mother would each *think* she was in charge.

I followed up with Katie, praising every small detail
And laughing at the thought of leaving this to any male.

I took it one more step and said when she was Adam's wife
We'd be so thrilled at last to have a daughter in our life.
It takes so little effort; just some carefully timed tears.
It's worked on Adam's father more than thirty-seven years.

It's sad that mothers never get the credit they are due
We thanklessly all save the day—such unsung heroes, true.
But that's okay, my Adam's on display for all to see.
Besides, I do not like it when the spotlight is on me.

The service nears completion, prayers and vows already said.
Let's turn our ear toward Father Tim and hear what's in his head:

Priest
I thought this day would never come; my nerves are almost shot.
Most weddings are quite punishing, but this one was a lot.

And holy shit these mothers make Bridezillas all look tame.
They wrangle and manipulate without a hint of shame.

Their husbands both look weary and just wish it all were done.
If having sex means wives like these, I think I'll stick with none.

I'm so relieved that next week has no weddings in the book
There's just one easy funeral, and then I'm off the hook.

You'd think the challenge just as big; it can't be any fun.
That's true, of course, except the challenge is reduced by one.

Oh sure, there's still a family to make things really tough.
But the person in the casket never gives me any guff.

The bride and groom are man and wife, it cannot be undone.
As if to prove that point, we find they even think as one:

Bride and Groom
I'm so relieved we made it after all that we've been through.
Our stubborn, pushy mothers somehow never had a clue…

That all of their "suggestions" we were doing anyway.
To keep the peace, it simply was a game we had to play.

For now, we must enjoy the calm; it won't be long 'til when
They find out that we're pregnant and the ruse begins again.

~ The Prompt ~

Category:
Rhyming Short Story

Genre:
Rom-Com

Theme:
Stubborn

Emotion:
Relief

The House Always Wins

I have come up with the perfect smart watch app. Instead of steps it counts hugs, and it tallies how many times you hear "so sorry for your loss," "you're in my thoughts and prayers," "if there's anything I can do, just call," and my personal favorite, "it was all in God's plan."

Well, folks, in truth it was all in *my* plan, but I'll get to that soon enough. For now, I'm counting down the last two hours of this wake. My feet are killing me and I'm sick of being comforted. The only good thing about the line of mourners is that they mostly block my view of the video screens. It was bad enough I had to find all the pictures of Henry for the memorial display; must he stare back at me on a continuous loop?

"Yes, it was so sudden," I respond to another of Henry's nameless coworkers. Since it's been a few minutes, I repeat a version of the line that's bumping me up on the canonization short list. "But we should be thankful no one else died from this terrible tragedy."

Nameless gives me a second hug for my selfless attitude and moves on. Yep, there's a lot to be thankful for.

After tomorrow's funeral, Henry's cremains will occupy a niche in the church's columbarium beside his parents, and I will bid all three of them a jubilant and eternal farewell.

I didn't always feel this way. I'm willing to bet most wives who kill their husbands would say the same. "Willing to bet." There's a Freudian slip if I ever heard one. You see, Henry being "willing to bet" caused all of this.

We were both nearing forty when we met at a mutual friend's "Y2K Complacent" New Year's Eve party in 1999. We really hit it off and shared our first kiss (and mutual smugness) at midnight when the lights stayed on and the world didn't come to an end.

Like my head, the world was still spinning when Henry took me home in a cab at 4:00 a.m. and I invited him in. He never really left. We were drunk, yet everything seemed so clear. We had each put our personal lives on hold in favor of our careers—I was a scientist and Henry a stockbroker. Though unspoken, we knew we likely missed the window of opportunity for children, and that was okay. We were enough for each other. We married that May.

Unlike struggling young newlyweds, we each had our own money and kept our personal finances separate. We created a third household account to which we both contributed. At Henry's suggestion, he managed that money, as well as all our independent investments.

A scientist works with facts, and the fact was Henry was good with money. Unfortunately, I'd forgotten that sometimes experiments blow up in your face.

I had lost half a million dollars when I finally got wise. I have no idea how many boxing matches, roulette tables, horse races, and other "sure things" that represented. No matter: clearly, Henry had only heard the "for richer" part of our vows. I'd listened carefully. Including the part about "in sickness and in health."

That's how we ended up at the Destiny Casino two weeks ago. As a (unbeknownst to me) VIP member, Henry had received a special invitation to the Grand Re-Opening of their Epic Buffet. Pre-COVID, even non-gamblers had come from far and wide to immerse themselves in this gastronomical extravaganza. Thanks to the passage of time and "unparalleled safety measures," the casino won approval to bring it back. Henry proposed it as a unique date night, and I accepted. He had no idea how unique it would be.

As a scientist, I knew the tools at the disposal of law enforcement. Henry's death needed to be a tragic, but explainable, result of an event that seemed to have nothing specifically to do with him.

Have I mentioned my area of specialty? Research biology. I'm willing to bet (oh, there I go again) you didn't know how easy it is for someone in my position to obtain Salmonella bacteria in a liquid suspension. Or how easy it is to discretely add it to a big vat of ranch dressing—Henry's favorite—when there are hundreds of people creating a distraction. Well, almost as easy as logging on to Henry's computer and making sure all his accounts were properly set up as payable-on-death to me.

I really enjoyed that VIP night at the Epic Buffet. The nearly three hundred people—Henry included—with projectile vomiting and bloody diarrhea later that night, not so much. Luckily for most, it was just a bad twenty-four hours or so. A couple of people ended up in the hospital but recovered. Everyone but Henry.

Three thousand people a year die from food poisoning in the United States. Officially this year it will be three thousand one… but that's bad data.

Salmonella didn't kill Henry. It just gave me the opportunity to take extra special care of him "in sickness," as promised. First, I made sure he took his insulin. I dialed up an extra big dose before I put the pen in his hand and helped him push the plunger.

Then, I thought swabbing the inside of his dehydrated mouth with something cool and moist would be helpful. We don't usually have shellfish in the house, what with Henry's deadly allergy, but just our luck I'd bought shrimp that day! I was able to get enough Pepto in his mouth to cover the smell before his throat closed all the way and I called 911.

May I confess something else? All this talk has given me a little case of gambling fever myself. When we were walking through the casino after dinner that night, I passed a slot machine called The Merry Widow. Somehow, I think that might be the game for me.

~ The Prompt ~

Category:
Flash Fiction

Genre:
Culinary Catastrophe

Character:
Gambler

Object:
Photograph

Buzz Kill

Kelly's fingers drummed the steering wheel as she inched down Lake Shore Drive, unable to escape the incessant buzzing.

Outside, it came from high-speed military aircraft, materializing from the mist of Lake Michigan to zoom between skyscrapers with terrifying inches to spare before blasting out over the water, all in a matter of seconds.

But it was the buzz inside that scared Kelly… the low rumble of two toddlers and a six-year-old who were well past their breaking point and could blow at any moment. *VIP parking my ass. Next time work on getting me to the damn place.*

Another jet seemed to skim the top of the minivan, and Joey pointed up and said, "Daddy!"

"No, honey," his mother answered. "Daddy isn't in that plane. He'll be in a plane in the big show later."

"The big show," she grumbled to herself. Another chance to play the loyal Blue Angel Wife (she preferred the more accurate "Blue Angel Widow," but that term made some of the ladies uncomfortable). Soon everyone would be telling her how wonderful and talented Grant was. *Talented my ass.*

"While he was picking lint off his dress uniform at the field, who was getting three kids presentable and into the car by herself?" her whispered monologue continued. "Synchronized flying? Try one-handed diaper changing on your lap in a bathroom stall while holding onto a three-year-old with the other."

"What, Mommy?" Joey asked.

"Nothing, honey," Kelly answered. "I'm just thinking out loud. Hey, look! I see the Ferris wheel. We're almost there." *Thank God for small favors.*

Once parked, she started unloading and flipped open the double stroller, which wobbled precariously on the front right wheel. *You had one job, Grant. One job.*

Kelly grabbed a screwdriver from the portable toolbox and tightened the wheel with the speed and precision of a pit crew. *He probably doesn't even know we have a toolbox in the van. Jeez.*

This latest crisis averted, she loaded the toddlers into the stroller and instructed Joey to hang on to the side. She put on a happy face for the elite gathering of families that lay in wait for her.

"Kelly!" one of the other wives shrieked. "You just missed the guys on their practice flyover, just for us. Grant was out in front and it was sheer perfection!"

This elite "flight demonstration squadron" of the Navy is comprised of just seventeen volunteer officers, with only five performing at a time. Four of the five rotate, but for the last three years, Grant has always been their lead flyer. This celebrity status has made him an icon, even among the other fliers' wives, and Kelly is often the recipient of the teenybopper-esque squeals of the members of his unofficial fan club.

But for all the minutia they could rattle off (birthplace: Seattle; favorite color: sky blue, of course), there are certain things only a wife knows. *Top secret security clearance my ass. You can't prevent pillow talk when the agent talks in his sleep.*

At first, Kelly thought it was just gibberish. Some of the words didn't even sound like English. Because they weren't.

The Russian was easy to pick out, but it took a while for her to realize what she thought had been burrito-induced moaning was Mandarin.

Knowing that web browsing at home was out of the question, Kelly further polished her dutiful housewife persona by bringing the kids to story time at the library. While the other Stepford Wives were reading *Soap Opera Digest*, she was using her precious free time to rendezvous with a new friend named Rosetta Stone.

It was apparent that Grant had been leading this double life for quite some time and that he was never going to let Kelly in on the secret. *That's okay. Everybody has secrets, right?*

Kelly continued to decipher what information she could, keeping it in the same hiding place where abused wives squirrel away a few bucks from the weekly grocery money until they have enough to escape for good.

This secret stash helped her endure days like today. That, along with the beautiful Navy Pier surroundings, glorious weather, and–miraculously–no outbursts from any of her kids, put a spring in Kelly's step as they made their way back to the van.

When all the kids and gear were loaded, she distributed their headphones and put a DVD into the player. All three were instantly mesmerized, and Kelly mirrored their look, alternating her trancelike stare between the glove compartment and the lakefront. A vibration from her watch broke the reverie. *Right on time.*

Almost simultaneously a huge explosion rocked the area, and a fireball appeared above the lake. Kelly's expression did not change, but she reached into her purse and pulled out a key, just as something in the glove compartment began to, of course, buzz.

She reached in, punched a code onto the compartment's false back, and pulled out the phone.

"Good afternoon, gentlemen," Kelly said, first in perfect Russian followed by perfect Mandarin. "As you no doubt know already, the American agent has been eliminated, along with the risk to your two fine countries. I am pleased I could provide the information you needed to accomplish the operation, and I await your instruction for my next assignment."

After some obligatory pleasantries, the callers disconnected. Kelly stowed the phone in its hiding place and watched as dozens of emergency vehicles rushed to the lakefront. *Good luck, fellas. You aren't going to find much.*

She looked back at her children, deeply enthralled and sweetly oblivious to the world around them. She put on her sunglasses and pulled out into the new day she had just made for herself.

Blue Angel Wife my ass. Now I'm a Blue Angel Widow whether they like it or not.

~ The Prompt ~

Category:
Short Story

Genre:
Spy

Setting:
Air Show

Object:
Toolbox

Justice for Abigail

I take my usual spot on the park bench, just like every morning. The blinding sunlight belies the chill in the late October air, so I zip my light jacket and hug myself against the bracing wind. I don't mind the cold. My heart and soul are numb, why not my body as well?

It's nearly two years since Abigail was killed. My first grandchild and namesake, she was the light of everyone's life, and I will never come to grips with her death.

She was thirteen on that Halloween night, and the group of eighth graders knew it was likely their last year of trick-or-treating. No one could have imagined why it would be Abigail's.

Ten years earlier, her mom was away on business, so I got to be her escort. My son fashioned a wicker basket around the stroller and Abigail was Toto to my Dorothy. Halloween was always my favorite holiday. Now I loathe it.

She and her friends went as a rainbow of crayons that horrible night. They walked in ROY G BIV formation, Abigail at the far left in red. It was well past sundown as the group turned a tight corner just as the drunk driver misjudged the turn and jumped the curb. The orange crayon had a broken leg; Abigail was dead.

I get up and walk across the expanse to the fence that runs parallel to the country road. Another rainbow in an autumn palette swirls and crunches beneath my feet. The trees are doing the fake dance of death they perform each fall. But their soon-to-be barren branches will come alive again in spring. I have no such hope for my spirit.

Across the road is a cornfield, ears picked and stalks waiting to be mowed down. Mowed down. Sounds like a job for a drunk driver.

I turn and look down the road, another part of my daily ritual. Just off the shoulder there is a white cross in the ground, adorned with flowers, pictures, and one Mylar balloon whipping in the wind—a makeshift memorial to another person gone too soon thanks to vehicular homicide. I'm sure there is something similar at the scene of Abigail's murder. I haven't yet been able to go back and look for myself. This is the best I can do for now.

I'm startled by a loud bang behind me and turn. Of course. It's Wednesday. The garbage truck is redepositing the dumpster back in the corral. Why does it surprise me? I should be used to loud thuds by now. It's the same noise I hear every night.

The nightmare never varies. Seven girls are a rainbow of joy strolling down the sidewalk, my beloved Abigail in red on the end near the street. Some have their arms linked; others are looking at their phones. I can't make out what they are saying, but laughter—everything from giggles to gales—fills the air.

Suddenly, just as they round a corner, the squeal of tires overwhelms any other sound. Abigail turns around and her face is frozen in a scream of terror. The car never slows and hits her with a sickening thud.

The car continues across the grass and crashes into a tree. The friends rush to Abigail and the girl in orange. Abigail is still. Spilled candy litters the pool of blood expanding beneath her like a cruel extension of her costume. Her eyes are wide and her mouth is open in a silent scream that I finish as I jolt awake each morning, sobbing and in a cold sweat.

There is no one on earth I detest more than the person who killed my granddaughter. She took Abigail's life and ruined mine and my family's. Turns out she was a big fan of Halloween. So much so, in fact, that she couldn't resist a little celebration on the way home. Her "little" celebration made her blow three times the legal limit on the breathalyzer.

Oh yes, she lived. My beautiful granddaughter is dead and her killer is alive. But don't worry. I will make her pay if it's the last thing I do.

I wipe fresh tears from my face as an air horn sounds behind me. I start back across the yard to the prison with the rest of the inmates.

I'll be out in six months, but that means nothing.

Living with the fact I drove drunk and killed my own granddaughter is a life sentence.

~ The Prompt ~

Category:
Short Story

Story must touch on this topic in some way:
The thud was unmistakable.
He slammed on the brakes and jumped out. Nothing.
Panning his eyes across a small field of corn, with red and orange leaves showering down from the nearby forest,
he shivered in his thin jacket. He then turned back
toward his truck and starting blinking wildly…

If the Shoes Fit

Brian stood amid the glitterati. His canonization had commenced; stained jacket, sweaty brow, and pungent essence notwithstanding.

It was New Year's Eve, and Gary Xagas, host of the most exclusive party in town at Chicago's most exclusive restaurant, Sheen, had brought out the renowned chef to take a bow.

More at home in front of a stove than a microphone—and well aware that Gary's show was more for Gary's benefit than his own—Brian's humble response was as genuine as the saffron in the gougères as the crowd chanted his name.

"Bri-an. Bri-an. EARTH TO BRIAN."

Jostled from his memory, Brian saw a waiter standing before him with an empty tray.

"We need more lobster empanadas," he said, "and Mr. Big is looking antsy, so anything might set him off."

"I wouldn't worry too much about Mr. Big," Brian replied, taking a pan from the warmer. "Why don't you take a break? I've got this."

Brian refilled the tray, grabbed a handful of cocktail napkins, and went through the butler's pantry into the festivities.

Gary's guest list had expanded from a year ago to fill the magnificent living room of the penthouse, a theater-in-the-round for the panorama of the Loop and beyond. Millions of lights dazzled from the skyscrapers and the streets far below, and the unmistakable radio spires atop the Sears Tower (real Chicagoans will never call it anything else) glimmered with seasonal red and green lights at their peaks.

There was inky darkness out the east window, with only an occasional blip in the distance to indicate it was not a black hole to another dimension. Normally, it took sunrise to ignite a shimmering light show on the crashing waves of Lake Michigan, but tonight those blips would become launching pads for spectacular fireworks, and the revelers had the best seats in the house.

Gary was standing next to Rosie McKenzie and both watched Brian approach a small group to offer the appetizer tray.

"What a difference a year makes," Rosie said. "To think last year, he was one of the top chefs in the world. Now he's catering parties."

"Well, not just *any* party," Gary said, giving her elbow a playful nudge.

They both smiled. "Of course," Rosie demurred. "Do you know what happened?"

"His wife had some kind of serious health problem; I don't know exactly what. At some point, he had to leave Sheen to take care of her. That's why I felt it was my duty to hire him for this event."

Rosie nodded. *Oh boy. He just doesn't miss an opportunity, does he?*

"How is she now?"

"I think she's still alive," Gary answered distractedly. Once he'd found the opportunity to pat himself on the back, he lost interest in the topic. "But enough about the help. I can see life is treating you great, Miss Big TV Star."

Rosie was in her eighth year as on-air weatherperson for the ten o'clock news on Channel 7, the ABC affiliate in the number three market in the country. Her face looked down on commuters from billboards and was plastered on the sides of buses like barnacles on a public relations battleship.

"Well, 'Big TV Star' is a bit of a stretch," Rosie replied.

"No way," Gary insisted. "Who wouldn't love to be in your shoes? I've heard rumblings that the network is interested. Soon you'll be shaking the windy city dust off your boots and moving to greener pastures. That won't surprise anyone a bit. Oh, look. Gene just got here. Will you excuse me, Rosie?"

Gary bolted before Rosie could answer, leaving her alone with her thoughts.

My shoes? I have news for you. The heels are too high and they hurt my feet. Greener pastures. The big time. That's what everyone thinks I want. Little do they know. I am so sick of these parties and phonies like Gary. I wanted to be a real meteorologist, not an on-air Barbie doll. Not a dressed-up mouthpiece for the station, being told where to go and what to do on what's supposed to be my own time.

She took a sip of the exquisite wine and closed her eyes.

One good day. I've had just one good day on the job. August 21, 2017. Benton, Illinois, to cover the total solar eclipse. And even then, no respect. They ignored my proposal for a prime time special about it; didn't want me wasting time going to schools. This was one of only six full solar eclipses in the entire first half of this century, and they were more concerned with what I was wearing on air than the event itself!

Rosie could feel her heart racing and took a couple of deliberate deep breaths to calm herself. She took another sip of wine and caught another glimpse of Brian.

At least I don't have to try to make a living bowing and scraping, serving preening snobs. Anyway, two more years and I'll have enough money to leave this all behind. Oh, shit! Here comes another poser blowhard. Turn on that perky weather girl charm. Just two more years. Focus on that. Just two more years.

"Jerry! You look fantastic. Things must be great at the museum."

Brian continued to make the rounds, politely offering overpriced hors d'oeuvres and ignoring the looks, which ran the gamut from condescending all the way to pitying. He didn't need superpowers to hear their thoughts: *Thank God we aren't in HIS shoes.*

He circled back toward the kitchen, past two guests discussing the host.

"Gary really pulled out all the stops tonight. I didn't think he could top last year's party, but he has."

"Too bad Lisa couldn't be here to share in the glory with him. I guess when duty calls, the chairman of the board and heir to the throne must answer. Even on New Year's Eve."

"Can you imagine being either half of that power couple? Jesus, it must be nice."

They glanced at Gary, apparently on a break from working the room, and clearly deep in thought.

So far, so good. These idiots are so busy kissing my ass they have no idea I've lost everything. They think Lisa is just off on one of her big shot, daddy's girl business trips. They don't know she's left me and taken daddy's money with her. Thank God I could transfer money to my Cayman account before the banks closed for the holiday. I have two days to figure out what to do next. And that goddamn Brian had to insist on a 50% deposit in cash. Well, the rubber check in his pocket will show him. I don't care what kind of family tragedy he's had. I've lost a lot more.

Gary looked up and saw Paul Atkinson, one of Cook County's foremost prosecutors, approaching. *Now there's a friend I should make.*

"Counselor, great to see you!" Gary gushed. "Looks like the city's scumbags are safe tonight."

"Good to see you too Gary." His handshake was powerful. "This party would be all over the society pages, if they still existed." He lowered his voice. "Hey, is that the chef from Sheen serving appetizers?"

Gary gave a grim nod. *Time to lay it on thick.*

"Yes, it's a sad story. Family illness and now it's come to this."

"Well, it's like they say," Paul noted. "The bigger they are, the harder they fall."

"But for the grace of God, we could all be in his shoes," Gary said.

Who'd want his shoes? They're ratty, and he probably can't afford to replace them.

"Just glad I could do my small part to help him out. Enjoy the party." They shook hands again and Gary sought his next prey.

Hello. Donald and Janet Giordano. I don't know if he can do anything for me, but it's always worth it to get close to that piece of ass. She'd be a great replacement for Lisa, but she'll never leave him. She's got it too damn good. Some guys get all the breaks.

Gary strode over, hand outstretched. "Glad you could make it, Don."

"Happy to be here," the charismatic stockbroker replied.

"And Janet," Gary cooed, leaning in a little closer than necessary to kiss her cheek. "You are looking especially lovely tonight." Only a trained eye could catch Don's glare. Janet's did.

"Looks like the big board is treating you well, Don," Gary continued, his gaze still on Janet.

Those diamonds must be worth a quarter million. They could solve all my problems. I always wanted to strip her down to the bare bones. This is another good reason to do it.

"Can't complain," Don said, putting an arm around Janet in a way that made it clear she was his and his alone. He gave her arm an ostensibly affectionate squeeze, right where the bruise hidden by her sleeve hadn't quite disappeared.

Keep your distance, Gary. I can't hurt you, but she will pay if this flirting keeps up.

"You look like you're ready for the Oscars red carpet with all that bling, Janet," Gary said, his gaze shifting between her necklace and cleavage.

"You have to break out the good stuff for the party of the year," Janet explained with a coquettish air. Don tightened his grip on her arm. "We need to ring in the new year in style."

New year is right. New year and new life. This jewelry—what you can see and what you can't—is my ticket to freedom from this monster.

Janet went over the plan for what seemed the millionth time.

Right after midnight, I'm going to pretend to visit the ladies' room and slip out. My mother and the social worker—the one holding my sworn deposition and photographic evidence of the abuse—will be waiting downstairs with Quentin. Tomorrow we'll have vanished, with new names and an unlisted address. So, get a good look at these tits, Gary. You and Don will never see them again.

Brian stopped at the trio, this time with a tray of champagne flutes.

"Mr. Xagas, the pianist asked me to let you know we're about five minutes from midnight, if you wanted to say a few words."

Has he ever turned that down? I don't think so.

Gary ignored Brian, grabbed a glass of champagne, smiled at the Giardanos, and made his way to the raised platform.

Brian walked to the kitchen with his empty tray. He grabbed a bottle of water and assessed the situation. Cleanup was well underway, and Rodrigo, his second-in-command, looked to have things under control.

"I can take it from here, boss," Rodrigo said, ever the mind reader. "Go ahead and beat the rush. No sense being on the road with the amateur drinkers. You have a lot to get home to."

"You sure?"

"Absolutely."

A fortissimo piano fanfare rung out from the other room and the crowd began counting down.

"Ten, nine, eight..."

"Happy New Year, boss."

"Seven, six, five..."

"Same to you, buddy. And don't kill yourself here. He'll probably make his regular staff clean it all again tomorrow anyway."

"Four, three, two, one."

The living room erupted and the two men shared a bear hug.

"See you next weekend," Brian said. "The Emerson shindig."

Rodrigo groaned, and Brian gave him a comforting pat on the shoulder.

"We'll live."

He grabbed his coat and went out the back door to the service elevator. He stepped into the alley and cheering could be heard echoing from and between the skyscrapers. The heavens were alive with fireworks.

As he stopped at the exit from the service lot, he noticed a nondescript sedan—one a person couldn't identify later if their life depended on it—pull up to the awning at the front of the building. The back door opened, and a young boy who looked about six years old jumped out and ran to a woman in a long fur coat and evening gown. Both got back into the car, and it pulled away. A tiny feeling of recognition was there and gone in an instant, and Brian turned onto the street for his short drive home.

Brian turned the key in the door and found Stephanie sitting on the couch, watching the fireworks out their eighteenth-floor window, a baby at her breast.

"Happy New Year," he said, leaning in strategically for a kiss. "Round One or Round Two?"

"Noah went first and Emma is almost done," she said. "How was the party?"

"The usual," Brian said. "Lots of sad looks for poor Brian."

They both laughed. They knew their situation had been the topic of much whispered speculation, but only they knew the true story.

Stephanie's "medical crisis" had been a high-risk twins pregnancy. Brian had hoped the owners at Sheen would be understanding, but they were more concerned with profiterole than preeclampsia.

So, Brian quit. His job had been a labor of love, not essential to their survival. After all, Stephanie had a six-figure job in the advertising industry. She took her fully paid leave, safely delivered their twins, and let Brian take over as Mr. Mom when she went back to work.

And it wasn't her using her maiden name that had kept Gary and his ilk in the dark… it was because they just couldn't be bothered. Brian still loved to cook, so he took the occasional high-paying gig for fun. If his hifalutin clients thought the view was good looking down their noses at him, it was even better from his vantage point.

He went to the fridge and pulled out the bottle of champagne. He popped the cork, filled two glasses, and returned to the living room.

"Stop working already and sit down," Stephanie pleaded. "After a night like this, your feet must be killing you."

"No, they're fine," Brian assured her. "The secret is being in the right shoes."

~ The Prompt ~

Category: Short Story

Character: Chef

Setting: New Year's Eve

Must include: Solar eclipse

~ Acknowledgments ~

This book would be incomplete without recognizing the people to whom I owe a tremendous debt of gratitude.

The members of the Plano Writers Group, a small band of talented and delightful folks who gather at our library to listen to each other's stories and offer kind but truly constructive criticism. A masterclass in creative writing couldn't teach me what I've learned from these treasured colleagues and friends, and I can unequivocally say this book would not exist without their *(cough)* prompting. A special shout out to Carl Armstrong, who generously (and extremely patiently) shared his expertise about the mechanics of getting this book to print.

My other writer pals, especially Dana Starr—my contest partner in crime. If misery loves company, I'm in great company indeed.

All the friends over the decades who never stopped believing in and encouraging me and my writing. You now have your answer to that infernal question, "When are you writing your book?"

My awesome family, immediate and extended, who have fortified and inspired me. My daughters Rachel, Sammi, and Becky not just observed but allowed me to be both mother and writer during their formative years. I hope that example is a small part of the reason they are such strong and amazing women today.

And finally, my husband Mike. His love and support are unwavering and unconditional. I couldn't, and wouldn't want to, do this without him.

~ About the Author ~

Laurie O'Connor Stephans lives in a far western suburb of her birthplace, Chicago (aka the greatest city in the world). By day, she works at a law firm. By night (when not fighting crime), she exercises her writing muscles in favor of the real ones. Most of her fiction features humor and twist endings, while she observes real life on the pages of her website blog, *We B Late*.

She and her husband, Mike, share their empty nest with two ridiculously entitled dogs that (most days) they wouldn't trade for anything in the world. She credits their harmonious forty-plus years of marriage to the shared joy of grandparenthood, and not the catharsis that comes from killing off characters whose resemblance to actual ~~husbands~~ persons, living or dead, is purely coincidental.

Laurie loves theater (especially musicals), the Chicago Blackhawks (and hockey in general), reading (of course), puzzles (crossword and jigsaw), games (especially trivia), and watching *Jeopardy* ("I'll take overuse of parentheses for $1,000, Alex").

Once a Prompt a Time is her first book.

~ About the Cover Artist ~

Award-winning artist, writer, and graphic designer Christopher Cudworth's work includes a Top 5 Cream of the Crop Poster Design from Runner's World magazine and Fine Art posters for The Farnsworth House and the Kane County Cougars baseball team.

He is the author of books on caregiving, theology, and environmental sustainability.

His website is Christophercudworth.com

Email: cudworthfix@gmail.com

For further information or to contact Laurie,
please visit her website:
https://LaurieOConnorStephans.com

Please leave a review on the website or at:
Goodreads: https://tinyurl.com/yndj4fv2

Please follow Laurie on social media:

https://www.facebook.com/LaurieOConnorStephans

https://www.instagram.com/laurieoconnorstephans/

https://www.threads.com/@laurieoconnorstephans

https://x.com/LaurieOCS

https://www.linkedin.com/in/laurieocs/

Once a Prompt a Time is also available
in hardcover and as an ebook.

Order here: https://a.co/d/0fe6up0H

www.ingramcontent.com/pod-product-compliance
Lightning Source LLC
Chambersburg PA
CBHW021446140726
48132CB00027BB/137

* 9 7 9 8 9 9 5 0 5 7 6 0 4 *